the
secrets
we keep

the secrets we keep

deb loughead

DUNDURN
TORONTO

Cover image: © JanLeoKaak/iStock
Printer: Webcom

Library and Archives Canada Cataloguing in Publication

Loughead, Deb, 1955-, author
    The secrets we keep / Deb Loughead.

Issued in print and electronic formats.
ISBN 978-1-4597-3729-7 (paperback).--ISBN 978-1-4597-3730-3 (pdf).--
ISBN 978-1-4597-3731-0 (epub)

    I. Title.

PS8573.O8633S43 2016   jC813'.54   C2016-903882-3
                                                  C2016-903883-1

1 2 3 4 5   20 ·19 18 17 16

Conseil des Arts du Canada   Canada Council for the Arts   Canadä   ONTARIO ARTS COUNCIL CONSEIL DES ARTS DE L'ONTARIO an Ontario government agency un organisme du gouvernement de l'Ontario

We acknowledge the support of the **Canada Council for the Arts** and the **Ontario Arts Council** for our publishing program. We also acknowledge the financial support of the **Government of Ontario**, through the **Ontario Book Publishing Tax Credit** and the **Ontario Media Development Corporation**, and the **Government of Canada**.

Care has been taken to trace the ownership of copyright material used in this book. The author and the publisher welcome any information enabling them to rectify any references or credits in subsequent editions.

—J. Kirk Howard, President

The publisher is not responsible for websites or their content unless they are owned by the publisher.

Printed and bound in Canada.

VISIT US AT

dundurn.com | @dundurnpress | dundurnpress | dundurnpress

Dundurn
3 Church Street, Suite 500
Toronto, Ontario, Canada
M5E 1M2

For Jack Livesley,
who always loves a mystery

1

OUR PRINCIPAL STEPS up to the mic and taps it. The sound, like a gunshot, makes me jump. My heart is hammering so hard everyone in the auditorium must be able to hear. How many other kids in the crowd are feeling as freaked out as I am right now?

"Sure glad I wasn't there that night," Aubrey says beside me.

"Yeah, lucky you. My parents still don't know I went."

I crane my neck, trying to figure out where Ellie is sitting. These days I try to avoid her as much as possible. But whenever she "needs" me, I have to be on call. I spot her one row back, sitting stiffly, hands clutching the armrest. When she catches my eye, she gives me a knowing smirk. I look away quickly.

At the podium Mr. Sinclair clears his throat.

"Thank you, students, for welcoming Ms. Stitski into our school. As you recall from last June, she and her family endured an unthinkable tragedy. She wishes to address the school today to express some of her ongoing concerns. I hope you'll all listen with respect and be brave enough to step forward if you feel you can help her in any possible way. Ms. Stitski."

A tall, slim woman crosses the stage to the microphone. She's dressed like a Banana Republic model, in a taupe jacket with rolled-up cuffs and black slacks. Her dark, cropped hair has a flash of grey along one side. She's a pretty lady, Kit's mom, but there's something else there, too. A shadowy veil seems to cover her features, concealing who she was before all this happened at the start of the summer.

She stands and stares out for a moment, the auditorium crammed with students from grades nine to twelve. I know from my experience in theatre arts that she can't see much; the bright stage lights are practically blinding. But she might as well be looking straight into my eyes. And reading my mind.

"I'm glad you could all be here today, and I thank Mr. Sinclair for permitting me to speak to you." A dramatic pause. She's obviously good at this. "I'm sure you all remember my son Kristopher, or Kit, as everyone called him, and the disturbing circumstances of his death."

Something twists in my gut as she says those words. I half-wish I could crawl under my seat to hide. Her voice is controlled, measured, as if she's standing in front of a court room addressing judge and jury.

"The coroner's inquest deemed it 'death by misadventure.' That verdict has been haunting me ever since. Because I don't agree. Something *else* happened that night. He did *not* wind up in the water by accident. I know that someone out there, one of the many who were at the quarry that night, knows more. Withholding that information could make you an accessory to a crime. It's in your best interest to step forward, and tell the police what you know to help all of us, especially Kit's brother and me, find some closure once and for all."

"God," Aubrey whispers. "She almost looks like she's about to cry, doesn't she, Clem?"

"Wouldn't you?" I say, blinking back tears and clenching my fists.

"I'm trusting someone will do the right thing, to help the rest of us heal." Ms. Stitski's neck tendons are standing out now. Her face has become a tight mask. "So many of you loved Kit, I'm sure, but a few of you were responsible for being cruel to him in the past. Teasing, bullying, call it what you want. But trust me, I know who you are. If you had *anything* to do with this …" she almost chokes on her words, "then step forward. And clear your conscience once and for all."

With that, Ms. Stitski abruptly spins and walks off the stage into the wings.

Instantly, the room fills with the buzz of a thousand bees. Mr. Sinclair hurries to the mic.

"Do your talking once you're outside. It's only ten minutes before last bell, but you're all dismissed for the day. Please leave in an orderly manner, and enjoy your weekend."

"She's talking about Spencer, isn't she?" Aubrey says, trailing me up the aisle to the exit. "I've heard stories. Kids are saying there was some sort of fight between him and Kit that night. Remember how he always gave Kit a hard time in middle school?"

Kids are saying. The thought is like a laser beam burning a hole in my brain. *Who* is saying? *Who* knows what?

Who'd believe anything — everyone.

"Yeah, but that was then and this is now," I tell her. "A lot has changed since then. And anyway, who knows what really happened that night? Maybe we'll never know for sure."

I can only hope.

Ms. Stitski is a lawyer at a local law firm. She knows how to dig out the truth, and she's on a mission.

The thought of what she might be able to find out leaves me almost breathless. Especially with Ellie keeping my secret.

And never letting me forget it.

"PIZZA'S HERE, CLEMENTINE," Mom calls from the kitchen that evening.

I've been hiding out in my room since I got home from school. Told my folks I was exhausted from a busy week. That's a bit of a stretch. I'm actually exhausted from a busy mind — one that won't allow me to think straight or concentrate on important things, like school work and theatre arts. Oh, and getting Jake Harcourt to notice me.

The way things are going, this is the new normal. Because guilt will not stop gnawing at me like a hungry rat. After this long, I almost had myself convinced that I was in the clear, that it was almost over. As if. But seeing Ms Stitski today made me realize that it will never end.

I force myself to walk to the kitchen and look happy about an order-in pizza.

"It's your favourite kind, honey," Mom says when I peek under the lid. "Lots of veggies and no anchovies."

"Thanks," I say. But the smell turns my stomach.

I take one piece and sit at the table. Zach's inhaling multiple slices in front of the TV screen, playing a video game. So I'm stuck alone with Mom and Dad, and no kid-brother buffer to distract them. Not that it's really nec-essary. Mom's watching a video on her iPhone and laugh-ing; Dad's reading something on his tablet and frowning.

I nibble my pizza slice and chew quietly, half-hoping they won't feel obligated to question me about my day the way a lot of parents would. But also half-hoping they might.

What I definitely need most right now is a friendly ear. I need someone to talk to, to help me figure stuff out about Ellie and every awful thing that's been going on between us. That used to be Mom — I used to be able to tell her anything. But this time, I'm too ashamed, too afraid of what she'll think of me. Plus she never seems to have much time to listen to me anymore.

Come to think of it, neither does Dad. They're almost always lost in their own virtual worlds — when they aren't stressing out about work, being super-busy teachers.

They're no worse than Zach and me, though. A fam-ily of techno-geeks who seem to rarely share actual face time. I've spent the last four months in misery, wallowing in my guilt, and they haven't even looked up from their screens long enough to notice. Might as well talk to the wall most of the time.

Because for sure the wall would make a better lis-tener than my parents.

WHAT TIME IS IT, CLEMENTINE?
I wake up from the nightmare hearing his voice. I'm gasping for air and fighting with my covers as though

I'm trying to break free. As though it's happening to me instead of him.

Nearly four months later, the awfulness still feels as fresh as if it just took place yesterday.

And I'm getting close to totally losing my mind.

I fumble for my phone on my bedside table and turn it on to check the time. It's 3:30 a.m., and there's a text message waiting for me. It's the middle of the night for god's sake. And then another message. *Three missed calls.* All from Ellie. An icy flash of fear washes through me.

Txt me as soon as you get this. She sent it at 2 a.m., when I was deep in nightmare land. The phone calls came right after.

This is not a good thing. Ellie insists that I leave my phone on all night in case she needs me. But tonight, before bed, I turned it off. I think I just wanted to stand up for myself for a change. Seemed like a good idea at 10 p.m., but now, in the wee hours, my decision is turning my stomach sour. Ellie will not be happy about this.

Sup? I text back. But I'm afraid to press send. I'm afraid of what might be up with her. I hate these middle-of-the-night surprises because I'm never sure what this girl, my so-called bestie, might have in store for me next.

Can I be bold enough to just shut off my phone and ignore the whole thing? Do I have the guts to do that, to come up with some lame excuse like my battery died? But she's already warned me about that. Said I should charge my phone every night, to be sure I don't miss a single thing.

I press send. I have to. I have no other choice.

Where WERE u Clem?????? I've been totally freaking out!!!!!! Her instant reply.

Why, El? What happened?

I'm with Mac. Mom doesn't know. Said I was going to ur place 2nite! U have to cover for me in the morning, k?

Which means I have to lie. To my best friend's mom. Because she lied to her first, and now I have to cover for her. This is the worst one yet.

Where r u? Why don't u just come here now?

Can't. Went for a long drive with Mac.

So what can I do?

If my mom calls tomorrow say I'm in the bathroom. Then text me, k?

And? How will that help? She'll just call your cell!!!!!

No, I'm turning it off. So I won't know if she called.

WHY!!!!!!!!

I just told u why!

But that doesn't make any sense.

Just do it Clem ☺ thnx xoxo

Smiley face. Like I *ever* feel like smiling when Ellie texts me these days. Like a smiley face makes everything okay.

Oh & if she shows up tell her I just left k?

WHAT!!!! Ur kidding right? If she shows up????

But she doesn't reply to that one. Just leaves me hanging as usual, stewing in my sweat, wondering if she's serious.

If her mom shows up in the morning, I'll be toast. What will I tell her?

Even though I'm getting better at lying, it still upsets me. But Ellie has it all figured out. She knows my parents leave early for the farmers' market every Saturday morning, so if her mom comes looking for her, at least mine won't answer the door.

Now and then, when her eyes aren't locked on her phone screen, Mom asks how Ellie's doing, and wonders why she doesn't come around anymore. I just explain that she's "madly in love" right now. And anyway, in high school everyone's way too busy to hang out all the time. Mostly, though, I keep my mouth shut and hold all the bad stuff inside. They don't know SO much!

On that awful night back in June, Ellie told her mom she was staying at my house, and I told my parents I was staying at hers. Then we rode our bikes over to the field party.

Everything changed the moment Ellie ran into Mac and started acting like I didn't exist. She'd had a mad crush on him ever since he was at our school, but back then he never even gave her a second glance. That night, though, he was all over her. I stuck around for a while, tried hard to have fun, but failed miserably. Finally I gave up, went home, and told my parents I'd been feeling sick at Ellie's. I got in trouble for leaving her house in the night, which was what they thought I did, and biking home alone instead of calling for a ride.

Ellie never even went home. After she met up with Mac that night, she tossed her bike in his trunk and drove around with him for hours. She's been driving around in that car ever since.

Her mother would flip out if she knew that. But Ellie has me to cover for her. And I have to, because she owns me. As long as I keep her secrets, she'll keep mine.

Like the fact that I was at that party. And that I may have been the last person to see Kit alive. That maybe he'd still be alive if I'd done the right thing.

Of course, Ellie's not the only reason why I can't let go of that night. Could I have saved Kit? It's that question that chews away at my dreams and wakes me up in fits of twisted blankets and regret.

Methought I heard a voice cry "Sleep no more!"

That line from *Macbeth* is an earworm that will not quit haunting me. Because it defines my current state of being. The voice is Kit's. It's like his ghost will *not* go away and leave me alone. And now that I know his mother's still hunting for answers, my secrets are spooking me even more.

2

SATURDAY MORNING I'M so uptight that I have a hard time devouring my bowl of chocolate Cheerios the way I always do before pouring a *second* bowl. And Zach notices, of course.

"What is *up* with you?" he says as he pours milk over his second helping. It's our new favourite cereal because of how the white milk turns to chocolate in the bowl.

"Nothing," I snap back, a dead giveaway. Meanwhile I have one eye on my phone screen the whole time, hoping that it won't light up.

"You are so full of it," he says. "Are you thinking about Jake again? Getting all nervous about the Sadie Hawkins dance? I bet anything you want to ask him."

Eeesh. How does he manage to bug me about stuff that's going on in my life when he's in eighth grade at middle school and I'm in high school? And why do I let it get to me? But ever since he overheard me blathering about Jake to Ellie on my phone last year, he's been giving me a hard time. And it totally bugs my ass.

"Maybe. And I'm not nervous about that at all," I lie. It gets easier and easier, really.

Everything about Jake makes me nervous. He's both cool and hot, with wavy blond hair and a lean, cut body.

Sometimes when he's near me, my tummy starts doing an "upside-down on a rollercoaster" thing that I try to ignore. Besides, I'd never stand a chance. The coolest girls in grade ten, and probably other grades too, practically drool on their designer running shoes whenever he's around. I'm sure at least one of them has already asked him out.

Back in middle school nobody really looked twice at Jake Harcourt — he was just the cute little skater dude, more interested in kick flips than girls, who were mostly way taller than him anyway. I was hung up on Jake even back then though. And I talked to him whenever I had the chance. I even pretended I was thinking of getting into skating, just so I could get closer to him. Then last year in grade nine, something suddenly changed. He had this crazy growth spurt, grew like an inch a month between September and June. Then he became a chick magnet. And everyone noticed, including me.

Back then, when some of us formed a Circle of Friends group in support of Kit, Jake was one of the first to sign up. Which attracted me to him even more. He had this kind disposition, and good nature. This willingness to be there whenever he could. He was so eager to help out Kit, he would even let him mess with his skateboard. Kit usually just fell over and laughed about it along with the rest of us. And it made me appreciate Jake even more.

I've noticed some other changes in Jake now, especially since the end of the school year. He's been hanging out with different kids, and rumours about him on social media are bouncing around like hailstones.

Especially when it comes to girls. I heard that he hooked up with three different ones this summer, just jumped from one to the next. But somehow, judging from those rumours, and from Jake's weird behaviour, he always seemed even more pissed off than the broken-hearted girls he dumped. That wasn't the Jake I remember. The sweet kid I knew from middle school. I hope the good old Jake is hiding somewhere underneath his lame new attitude. Because I seriously do not know who this guy is anymore.

And Zach is right. In spite of everything I've been hearing about Jake, I still want to invite him to the Sadie Hawkins, the only time of year when girls are "allowed" to invite guys to a dance. Geeky, artsy girls that are like me, anyway. Girls who might never get invited to a dance otherwise; girls who are no competition for the other cooler ones. But I doubt I'm up to asking him. I just don't have the guts.

When someone knocks on the front door, I completely forget about Jake. My spoon drops onto the table, and I nearly choke on a mouthful of cereal.

"You getting that or should I?" Zach says.

"Um… um …" I say, then swallow hard.

"Too slow," Zach says, then jumps up to answer.

I catapult out of my chair. "Wait! Hold it! If it's Ellie's mom, tell her we've both gone out somewhere!"

"What?" He stares at me and raises one brow. "It's like nine in the morning! Where would you have gone? And where's Ellie anyway?"

"Can you just do it?" I plead, but he shakes his head.

"Nope. Don't drag me into this. You do it yourself."

My legs are melting candle wax as I shuffle toward the door. How will I ever pull this off without giving myself away? Deep breath, phony smile, reach for the doorknob.

"Unless ..." Zach says behind me, and I freeze just in time.

"Unless *what?*" I mouth the words, so Ellie's mom won't hear from behind the door.

"Science test on Monday. Need help studying this weekend. Big time."

"That's so totally worth it," I say, then spin around and head for the bathroom to hide.

"Hey, Mrs. Denton," I hear my brother say just as I close the door to a crack. "It's good to see you again. It's been so long."

"Could I speak to my daughter, please?" Mrs. Denton sounds the total *opposite* of happy to see my brother. As if she can barely stop herself from yelling.

"You mean, Ellie?" Zach says. I can't help but smile, as nasty as the situation is. This kid, with his big brown eyes, does "innocent" well. Good luck to my parents with *that* kid.

"She's the only one I have," comes the *not* amused response. "She said she was here, but I keep calling her phone and she won't answer. Not my texts either. I need to tell her something. And since when has your family given up your landline? When I called I got a 'no longer in service' message."

"Yeah," Zach says. "We all have our own cell phones now, so my folks ditched our landline. No use paying for it anymore since mostly telemarketers call. At first they were —"

"Zachary." Mrs. Denton shuts him down mid-sentence. "*Where. Is. Ellie?*"

"Um … well … she's not here, and neither is Clem. They went somewhere, for a walk or run, or something, I think, so I —"

The door slams. Three seconds later Zach's peering at me through the crack.

"That went well," he says. "Seriously, what is *going on* with you two?"

"God, Zach, I wish I knew." I close the bathroom door and hope he believes me.

It wasn't always like this with Ellie and me.

Way back in kindergarten, when we first became friends, her life and mine were pretty much the same. We both had two parents and a brother, and we lived in bungalows a few blocks apart. Because both my parents were teachers, they had the entire summer off. And Ellie's parents made arrangements with mine for Ellie and her brother, Tommy, to spend every day with us, sort of like free daycare.

We would have been together anyway. We mostly spent those summers being schlepped around between swimming lessons and arts-and-crafts camps, and we had a blast. For ages we were one big happy family, until everything fell apart about two years back, when Ellie and I were thirteen.

It came out of nowhere. Ellie and Tommy's dad, who was a computer programmer, was transferred to the West Coast, and their mom decided she wasn't willing to go along. Ellie's mom wanted a stable life for her kids. She wanted to keep them in the same school, with the same friends. She also had no intention of giving up her own job running a chain of successful consignment shops, and trying to start over on the other side of the country. So she put her foot down and said no. She actually thought he'd change his mind, Ellie told me. But he didn't.

Even worse, Tommy decided to go along with him. He said he needed to be with his dad. Ellie said so, too, but her mom was pulling in the other direction. She was desperate for at least one of her kids to stay behind. And since she was a daddy's girl, that didn't sit well with Ellie. But she stayed in town, just to please her mom.

That was when everything started to change for Ellie. She discovered she had a bargaining tool and could get away with just about anything. When things didn't go her way, if her mom didn't give her money for clothes, or pay for a brand new iPhone, she'd threaten to leave. And I got dragged along for the ride.

Back in the kitchen I try to choke down the remains of my soggy cereal while madly texting Ellie. But she won't answer me either.

Her mom's on the hunt for her. Actually, Mrs. Denton is probably driving around looking for both of us. I start to panic, and feel like pitching my phone at the wall. Then finally, *finally*, a text pops up.

Coming over to pick u up. Be ready in 5 minutes.
What's going on?
I'll explain in 5 minutes.

"She's making me totally crazy!" I yell at the ceiling.

"How would we ever know?" Zach blurts from the family room, where he's playing a video game, as usual. "Anyway, you're the one who keeps on letting her *make* you crazy."

I stomp to the doorway to glare at him. "Don't you have some homework you should be doing?"

"Yup, and I'm waiting for you to help me. *Remember*?"

"Wish I could *forget*," I say as I run to my room to change out of my pajamas.

Five minutes later someone hammers on the front door again. When I fling it open, sure enough Ellie's standing there. Right on time for a change. She's a total mess: her mascara's made raccoon smudges under her brown eyes, her blond-streaked hair's all snarled, her jeans and T-shirt are crumpled like they've been slept in. Which isn't a stretch for Ellie. Mac's car is parked at the curb, rumbling and thumping.

"What the heck happened to *you*?"

"Don't even ask," Ellie says. "Just get into Mac's car, and hurry, okay?"

"Why? Your mom's been here looking for you, you know."

"I *know* that, Clem. Just get in the car, *please*, and I'll explain!" she says, dragging me out by the arm.

I push the front seat forward and climb into the back of Mac's old, blue Buick Wildcat. A refurbished classic, not that he did the work. His parents have money. This car was his grade twelve grad present last year. Apparently he's college-bound at some point, from what Ellie's told me. But she's younger than him. And totally gullible. And I don't like him at all.

"Hey," he says over his shoulder. "How's it goin' Clem?"

"Fine," I say. I sigh as I settle into the stiff seat.

The Wildcat jolts into gear as the stereo thumps out some hip-hop song that makes the whole car vibrate.

I'm sitting right behind Mac. I feel like giving him a slap upside the head for messing my friend up, for changing her so much.

Ever since Ellie's fantasies came true, and the two of them hooked up seriously at that field party, I've been losing respect for her. Apparently they're madly in love, and make a big deal of proving it. They even make out in public, which is totally gross. And now it's October, and those two are rocking their relationship, and meanwhile my life has been going down the toilet. I don't think I've ever liked anyone less than them. Our ten-year "best friendship" is pretty much history.

That's why it sucks so much that I've become a crucial part of their relationship. Because I'm the one who's always stuck cleaning up Ellie's muddy tracks. Every time she does something risky, I become part of the plot.

Ellie's mom despises Mac even more than I do. He hardly ever talks and he acts sullen, so I can't blame her for hating that her daughter spends so much time with him. A whole lot more time than Mrs. Denton even realizes.

Sure, Mac's sort of hot, in a dark-and-dangerous way, but it ends there. His personality is a big fat ZERO!

"So, what are we doing?" I ask, but I have a feeling I already know.

"Okay, so I talked to my mom, told her that I accidentally left my phone off."

"Yeah, like she'd believe that. Your phone is *always* on!"

"Just *listen*, will you?" she snaps over her shoulder. "I told her we went for a walk to the plaza and that we're both on our way back to our place now. That you're walking me home. So, Mac will drop us off near the plaza, and we'll take it from there."

What a humongous mess. "So how do you explain the way you look?"

"What do you mean? How do I look?"

"Check the mirror," I tell her.

She does and she gasps. "Crap. Okay, gotta do some maintenance on the face!"

Ellie whips a tissue out of her purse, spits on it, and starts to dab at the mascara. Next she has a brush in her hand and starts to fix her hair. I just sit in the back seat and shake my head. How can she stand living this way, always on the edge of getting caught? But I guess that gets easier, too, with practise.

"You look good to me, babe," Mac says. He grabs her and pulls her over and starts practically sucking on her face, right in front of me. *While* he's driving!

"Okay, you guys, there's the plaza. Stop the car, Mac," I tell him, desperate to get out of that cramped back seat. He pulls over to the curb, but not before swerving a bit to freak me out.

"Hope your mom won't be too pissed at you, El," he says, and he gives her another long, wet one. Yecch! *Why don't you just swallow her whole head?*

Then Ellie and I stand by the side of the road as he speeds off in his way-too-cool car. She just shakes her freshly brushed hair and sighs, like this is all such a huge inconvenience. For her.

"Let's go, Clem," she says. "And try not to look too guilty in front of my mom, okay? You're not so great at playing it straight."

Instead of walking on command, I stop on the sidewalk and stare at her.

"What are you waiting for?" she demands. "*Hurry*. I want my mom to actually *believe* this story, so we need to show up, like, *now*."

"Where were you last night?"

"Don't worry about it, Clem. We just went for a long ride, and Mac was too tired to drive back. We parked on a country road, so he could sleep for a bit before driving home."

"I'm totally sick of this. I don't know how you can't be yourself." I try not to blink, even though my eyes are suddenly full of tears.

Ellie tips her head and frowns, tries to look innocent. "Sick of what?"

"Everything. Of covering up for you all the time. Of telling lies. Of being glued to my phone in case *you* need something. Of always feeling like I owe you. I never should have listened to you that night and told all those lies to my folks, and snuck out to that stupid quarry. Just because you were hoping that Mac would be there."

"How come you sound so mad?" She has that quaver to her voice, like she might cry any second. It's one of her tricks to win me over. She's extremely good at crocodile tears. "And you kinda do owe me. I mean, look how much I've done for you. Just by *not* telling what happened."

I feel sick at her words. This is never, ever going away. I'm tired of wishing I could somehow make it un-happen, or that I could change the way things went down that night. But there's no turning back time, that's for sure.

I slap a wobbly, fake smile on my face. "Okay, let's go," I say, and I follow her home.

She texts all the way, doesn't even look at me. Keeps on sending messages to somebody else and laughing, then texting some more. Probably Mac. I hope he isn't texting and driving, the way he was kissing and driving a while ago. Hmm. If something were to happen to him, then maybe this rotten situation would finally change. And as crappy as it is to even think that way, I just can't stop myself.

Because that can't happen soon enough for me.

3

ELLIE'S MOM IS waiting for us in the doorway, arms crossed, in warrior stance.

"Don't think I can't figure out what's going on, you two," she yells from the doorstep. When we're closer, she grabs Ellie's arm, yanks her into the house, and slams the door in my face.

Ellie won't get into much trouble, though. She never does. She's great at laying on guilt trips about the way their life has changed. And if that doesn't work, she'll just threaten to move out west with her dad, and her mom will back right off.

I pass the plaza again on my way home from Ellie's. The place is a gathering spot for kids, and even this early on a Saturday morning you can find the skaters there, working on their tricks. A few guys have waxed the curb in the parking lot already, out behind the garbage bins where there's less of a chance that the shopkeepers will chase them away. They're practising their grinds and ollies, and I stop for a minute to watch.

Oh, god, Jake is there, too, dressed in his baggy skater pants and loose T-shirt, just like the others. When he spots me he skates right over, and my heart picks up speed.

"Hey, Clem," he says, and I grin even though I can barely breathe. Then he actually nudges me with his shoulder. The warm skin of his arm, the one with the spiderweb tattoo, touches my skin for a second and I shiver. "So, what're you doing here so early?"

"I just walked Ellie home," I tell him."

"Ellie Denton? She's going out with that dude with the amazing car, right?"

"Blue Wildcat." I scowl even though I'm trying hard not to.

Jake snaps the back of his skateboard with his foot, catches it in the air, and starts to spin one of the wheels. "My brother went to school with that dude. He was always a bit of a knob, way too full of himself."

"No kidding. I don't know what Ellie sees in him. Sometimes, I think she stays with him just to piss her mom off. He's a total creep."

Okay, so we're standing here talking like a couple of old friends, just like we used to in middle school. Should I ask him to the dance now? Before it's too late, before this conversation hits the wall? *Do it, Clem!* But I start to blush, and I can't get *any* words out. And maybe that's a good thing because what do we even have in common anymore? I still don't know the first thing about skateboards, so I can't even fake it.

"So, *anyway* …" I finally spit out, but then someone across the parking lot yells Jake's name. We both turn to look. Something seems to be going on, and one of the guys, Spencer, starts waving Jake over.

Jake holds up a finger. "Just one sec!" he yells. "So, anyway, *what*, Clem?"

This is the moment. This is my cue, and I know what I want to say next, if I can just suck it up and get the words out in the right order. It's no longer about the dance. Instead, I want to say exactly what I'm thinking right this second: *So, anyway, why are you still hanging with these losers?*

Like Spencer. In middle school, he used to give Kit a hard time way too often. He's probably the bully Ms. Stitski was talking about in her speech yesterday, just like Aubrey said after the assembly. To be fair, though, he really didn't bother with Kit in high school. He seemed to have outgrown it — there was cooler stuff to move on to, new kids to chill with, new shit to disturb. And so many new kids to harass. Smaller ones, geekier ones. The usual suspects.

He's become an even sketchier kind of guy, and from what I hear, he hangs out with the most "popular" (for questionable reasons) girls, the same ones who follow Jake around like his own private fan club. And Spencer is totally skateboard obsessed, says he hopes to get sponsored someday, and skips classes way too often so he can practise. I've got a feeling he's not being totally honest about that. Everyone knows he carries around a can of spray paint in his backpack and likes doing graffiti under bridges. He also likes hanging around some of the older skaters, a couple of high-school dropouts, and sharing their joints at the skate park.

Back in middle school, Jake never really had much to do with him. But for some reason, I see them together all the time now. Maybe it's just the skateboarding thing. I'm worried though — Jake seems so different these days. He's changed in a bad way. That sweet nature is gone and he seems pissed off a lot. So I decide to take a chance and throw it out there.

"Okay, so *anyway*, what's up with you and Spencer? You never used to chill with him before." While my heart punches away at my ribcage, I try to summon a look that's both earnest and concerned.

Jake shrugs. "I dunno. He's just into the same stuff as me, I guess. He's a wicked skater. Why do you even care?" he asks. "And what does it even matter to you? Spencer's okay, you know. Everyone talks shit about him. But you don't have to believe everything you hear." He looks away for a second.

I take a deep breath. We used to be good friends. I can do this. "Maybe it's just, well, you're not like him. Never were. And now it's almost like you're fixated on him or something."

"What's *that* supposed to mean?" A hint of frost now in his blue eyes.

My hands are all clammy. I can't handle the way he's staring at me, half angry, half hurt. I look up at the sky just as a sparrow swoops past. Right now I wish I could fly away, too. But it's a bit late for that. I can't un-say what just came out. And I have to say the rest because it's hanging in the air. "Well, it's just that it doesn't look so good on you, Jake."

Jake seems confused for a second. Then he frowns. "Okay wait a sec, I know what this is about now. That school assembly yesterday. You think …" he shakes his head, almost with disgust. "You think Spencer had some-thing to do with what happened, don't you? Just like Kit's mom does. Because of those freaking rumours someone's spread, about them fighting. Hell, maybe you even think *I'm* involved somehow."

"God, of course not, Jake. And I don't have a clue whether or not Spencer had something to do with it. All I know is that he was there, too. And he's kinda badass. You should watch your back, just in case. Shouldn't you?" His eyes narrow. *Uh-oh.* I might have crossed the line.

"Look," he says. "I know Ms. Stitski's on a mission. She wants to know what happened, and she's powerful enough to find out. But I was *there* that night. And I *saw* pretty much *everything* that happened." There's a defensive snarl in his voice. "And Spencer had nothing to do with it, no matter what anybody wants to say."

Does he really think I'm judging him when I'm just trying to show that I care? I can't believe how much I totally suck at this stuff. Jake glances over at Spencer, who's arguing with a shopkeeper out by the garbage bins now. I catch snatches of the yelling match, as Spencer tells the guy to get lost.

"It's not like we're bothering anyone back here, dude, and so what if we waxed the fuckin' curb? We always do this. So just chill, and act like we're not here." Spencer is right in the shopkeeper's face. Way too close. The shopkeeper takes few steps back and holds up his hands.

"Okay man, okay, I don't want any trouble," we hear him say. "But you're scaring off customers, and that's bad for business."

"Who gives a crap," Spencer tells him, laughing. "They'll just go elsewhere."

"So check it out," I say, pointing at the ruckus, which is getting worse as more skaters pipe up in scrappier voices. "That shop owner is going to go back inside to call the cops now. Do you *really* want to hang around with a jerk like that, who challenges anyone that gets in his way? This guy's like a disaster waiting to happen."

"Yeah, well don't believe everything you hear, Clem. Those rumours? I've heard them, too. Some asshole must have had a reason for spreading them, right? I mean, I really thought you were way cooler than this."

Jake drops his skateboard with a clatter, and rides over to the other guys. I feel like I've been punched in the stomach. I turn around so I won't see him heading in the wrong direction — away from me. Why didn't I just keep my mouth shut?

There's no way I feel like hanging around to see how things will end here. It all just leaves me feeling turned inside out, knowing Jake is part of it. That he's choosing to hang out with that jackass Spencer.

There's nothing left to do but wonder about it all as I wander slowly home. I mean, what happened just now with Jake, and with Ellie — what was that? Why can't things be like old times, fun times, the way they were just a few years back, like before Ellie's dad moved away. And since we started high school, things have gotten even worse. Our friendship just isn't the same anymore. But ever since that field party and Kit's death, there's no turning back. Just about everything in my life that means something has turned to crap.

The ghost of Kit trails along right behind me, asking all the same questions. How did it all go so very wrong? How has everything changed so suddenly and so drastically, and how has the happiness been sucked out of so many lives? Because that field party in June was supposed to be fun times, and it actually started out that way.

Word about the end-of-school bash had spread like wildfire. Then that night, around dusk, everyone met at the field on the edge of town, the one that backs onto the quarry.

My folks had always warned me about field parties, but I took the risk anyway. It sounded way too cool to miss out on. And what could have been a bonfire with a few kids from grade nine going into ten turned into a crazy party, with too many kids of all ages and too many bad things going on.

Kit Stitski showed up that night, too. And even though a bunch of us from middle school were there, his so-called Circle of Friends who always pitched in and tried to keep an eye on him, something went wrong , and he disappeared. It was too dark, too noisy. And in the end, too awful.

I'm about to turn a corner near my street when I hear it: the unmistakable sound of skateboard wheels clattering along the pavement. I look back at the very instant Jake zips through the intersection I just crossed, eyes straight ahead, not even checking to see if any cars are coming. As if he's in a huge hurry to get somewhere. Or maybe in a hurry to get *away* from somewhere. Is it possible? Did he listen to me back there at the plaza, change his mind about sticking around? Come up with an excuse to split?

A small smile starts to form on my face, along with a small flicker of hope in my heart.

THE REST OF the way home, and for the rest of that afternoon, sweet possibilities wrestle with sour realities. As much as I can hope and dream that something might happen between Jake and me, the memory of being at the quarry that night is like a painted backdrop in a play. I keep hoping for the curtain to drop.

While we sit at the kitchen table later that afternoon, Zach keeps on nudging me back to reality as I try to focus on helping him with science, as promised. Still my thoughts swoop away like an out-of-control kite, and crash into the blatant truth. *I'm* the one who let Kit leave that night. *I'm* the one who betrayed him.

I keep on reviewing that moment, over and over again, as if I'm practising lines for a scene in a play that I wish I didn't have a part in.

> **Act I, scene 1**: *At the party. Everyone dancing and drinking and carrying on around the bonfire. Much mischief and revelry. Kit runs up to Clem.*
> **Kit**: What time is it, Clementine? Time for me to pee! *(jumps about, legs clamped together)*
> **Clem**: Seriously Kit? *(Looks over shoulder toward Jake and party fun)* Okay, well there's a clump of bushes right over there. You'll find a spot.
> **Kit**: *(distressed)* Will you come with me? Please?
> **Clem**: God, Kit, I can't stand there while you're peeing. That's just gross.
> **Kit**: But, Clem, it's so dark over there.
> **Clem**: Come on, suck it up. You'll be fine, buddy.
> *Kit runs off toward bushes, Clem turns back to party, eyes scanning crowd for Jake.*

I will never forget that feeling of impending doom when I opened my eyes the next morning. Knowing that I'd forgotten something important. And knowing what it was the moment Mom walked into my bedroom without knocking first.

She stood in the doorway, her face twisted with distress, lost for words. Then she found them. "Kit's missing."

My first thought was like a boulder hitting me in the chest, knocking the breath right out of me — *it's my fault*.

At least my reaction seemed normal. I instantly burst into tears, and Mom hurried over to rub my back. And I couldn't say, "Did they check the quarry?" Because how would I have known he was there if I didn't go?

By then it was way too late anyway. Kit never made it home that night because he never left the quarry. They found him later that morning, drowned in the cold, black pond.

I only ever told *one* person about seeing Kit walk off into the dark. Ellie, my "best" friend. Now the two people I cared most about up until that summer night have completely changed. Jake, who I'd once called a good friend, has turned into someone I don't even know anymore. And Ellie's become a sneaky liar who blackmails her supposed best friend into doing anything she wants on threat of giving my secrets away.

The terrible truth is that deep down I know I've changed, too. I'm just getting better and better at denying it.

4

LATE SUNDAY MORNING we all head out for brunch, our monthly treat. The local café serves to-die-for crêpes, and our family needs a fix every now and then.

Mom, Dad, Zach, and I have all squeezed into the same booth. I'm totally antsy, jiggling my feet under the table as I wait for the server to deliver my fruit crêpe, piled high with a cloud of whipped cream and drizzled with chocolate sauce.

The rest of Saturday I never heard a word from Ellie. There are two possibilities for that. She's either been grounded, or she's mad at me for some reason or other. Lately she always finds reasons to be mad at me. Somehow I've become the person to blame for all her woes. And even though she's caught up in this big whirlwind romance, she's always crabby. Any minute I expect her to text me, needing something else.

It makes me feel twitchy. The cramped booth isn't helping, and I try to distract myself. My thumbs dancing as I switch between texts and Instagram to find out what was going on last night. Now and then Dad nudges me to move over, tells me I'm hogging the seat. I just laugh and nudge him back. Across from us, Mom and Zach are having the same nudging match, judging from their body language.

I didn't miss much last night. I stayed home and watched a movie on my laptop in my room, and most of my other friends did the same thing. That's because they all went to the Saturday matinee while I fulfilled my end of the bargain I made with Zach. Everyone was talking about the zombie rom-com on Twitter, and added rave comments about how awesome it was. I missed out, as usual, because of Ellie.

I snicker at a few things my friends posted about certain gruesome-but-funny scenes in the movie, meanwhile gritting my teeth because I'm the only one who didn't see it.

I watch a YouTube clip that somebody posted of a skateboard fail. I groan when the guy wipes out, then look up embarrassed that I'd groaned so loud. Nobody'd noticed.

And then the text from Ellie shows up and my stomach flips.

Something big is happening soon Clems!!!!!!!

Like what E?

Like Mac has these HUGE amazing plans for next weekend. And I need your help.

Suddenly I feel nauseous. Just the thought of food makes me sick.

What if I'm not available Ellie? What if I'm busy.

Oh you'll be available Clems. Love you xoxo ☺ You'll help me, right??????

I'm totally stunned by her announcement. I put my phone down and stare at it, wishing I could crush it under my shoe. I drum my fingers on the table, trying to get anyone's attention. Maybe it's time to come clean with my family and let them know what's going on. Maybe someone will have an idea about how I can stop this Ellie crap from destroying my life.

"Mom," I say, nudging her with my foot. "Can I ..."

"Just a sec, honey," she says, holding up one finger and staring at her phone.

"Dad? *Dad*?" He doesn't even hear me. The restaurant is noisy and of course he's staring at his screen. And Zach may as well not even be here either.

Nobody at my table has even noticed I'm in distress. They're all slumped over their own smartphones the exact same way I am. Except for Dad, who's using his tablet. It's been glued to his hands pretty much 24/7, ever since Mom gave it to him for his birthday in September. She secretly told Zach and me that he even falls asleep most nights with the thing on his stomach. He even takes it into the bathroom — gross!

Across from me, Mom sits in a daze, swiping her finger across her phone screen, and Zach's thumbs are flying as he plays some stupid game.

How pathetic can our family possibly get? When I glance around the room, most of the families with kids our age are doing the exact same thing, of course. Wired, logged on, hunched in the same sloppy positions, necks at weird angles, eyes focused on their screens. Completely ignoring each other. The only people talking to each other are much older. Maybe they aren't as hooked on technology as the younger generations, but still, a few of them have phones on the table, right beside their plates. They even check them now and then.

The only ones having fun are a few little kids. They're scrambling around in their seats, babbling to each other, scribbling with crayons on colouring sheets provided by the café. Their distracted parents are ignoring them, too focused on screens. It's utter craziness! I bang my fist hard on the tabletop.

"What is *wrong* with this picture," I say, loudly. Maybe even *extremely* loudly, because more than a few heads veer in our direction. "How can we ever know what's going on with someone, unless we actually look at them?"

"Clem, shh," Dad says beside me in his grumpy voice.

"*Why*, Dad? Am I disturbing you?" I stare at him, but he doesn't even look over at me. "Dad?" I nudge him hard. "*Hello* in there!"

I have Mom and Zach's attention though. They watch suspiciously from across the table, as if they're afraid that I might be totally losing it.

Dad finally looks up, too.

"What's your problem, Clem?" His eyebrows are stitched together in a worried way.

"Turn off your tablet, Dad. I dare you. Mom and Zach, too. Let's try talking face-to-face for a change."

"Yeah *right*, Clem," Zach says, then focuses on his phone.

"Seriously." I reach across the table and snatch it from his hand.

"Hey! Bite me, Clems," he yelps, grabbing it back. More heads turn. Mom cringes.

"I'm not kidding around," I tell them. "I just want to see if we can all do this."

Mom's half-smiling now. "Your sister has a point, Zach. A very good one."

I flash a grateful smile at her.

"We're not even talking to each other," I say. "It's pathetic. And look around. Most of the other families aren't talking either."

"That's because there's nothing to talk about," Zach says.

"Hold on," Mom tells him. "That's only because we haven't even tried. So let's all turn off our devices and have a chat."

"Have a *chat*?" Zach folds his arms against his chest and rolls his eyes. "That's what people do online, Mom. They *chat*. They message each other. You do it every day."

Dad starts laughing and actually puts down his tablet. "Chatting was invented long before the Internet, Zach. I agree with Mom and Clem. Let's try this."

"Sweet! Turn your phone off, bro," I say.

Zach narrows his eyes at me. "What's in it for you? You're *always* on your phone."

"Well, I guess I'm trying to change," I tell him. "Haven't you heard of Internet addiction? We're all turning into techno-zombies. Do you know that the first thing in my hand every morning is my phone?"

"Hmm, that sounds familiar," Mom says. "To be honest sometimes I even sneak a peek at school when my grade fours are doing seat work."

"Oh, me, too, Laura," Dad says. "We're all guilty, aren't we? We don't own our devices, they own us. Really, we should try to work on this."

Zach looks stunned. "You don't mean we have to give them up, do you, Dad?"

Dad's pause is so long that I start to get nervous myself. I may have an agenda here, but I don't want it getting out of hand. I'd honestly be lost without my phone.

"Not so much give them up, as put them down. What if we have no-phone zones at home and times when no electronic devices can be in use, including video games. And if we want to watch a movie, we all watch it together, so we can talk about it and share a bowl of popcorn."

"Yes, John. That's a great plan!" Mom leans across the table with gleaming eyes.

I'm not so sure I like that look. Am I creating a monster here? Still, I just sit and nod in agreement, even as Zach's kicking me under the table.

And right then my phone screen lights up again. Another text message from Ellie. I don't even check what she's saying because I already know what it will be about. And my mind is made up. I'm ending this now.

"We just have to set some guidelines and decide as a family what they'll be," Dad says. "Really, Clem, this is such a very thoughtful idea. I'm so glad you noticed how little attention we pay to one another lately."

"So, let's toss some ideas around," Mom says. "Right now. A brunch out as a family with phones turned off is a great place to start, isn't it? What else can we do to change our obsessive techno-geek habits?"

Zach looks queasy, like he's suddenly been stricken with the stomach flu. He mouths the words "thanks, stupid" at me, and I shrug and mouth back "you're welcome, moron."

Okay, so I haven't been completely honest with my family about my motives for this. But it's a win-win situation, as far as I'm concerned. Now I can tell everyone I know that our family is trying to limit our "wired" time. That we've made a pact to disconnect, which will be really good for the family. Now we can actually start connecting face to face. And during certain times of the day, nobody will be able to reach me. Including Ellie. I finally have a legitimate excuse for turning off my phone. All my own brilliant idea!

OVER BRUNCH IN the café, we came up with the new unplugged house rules. When we got home, Dad printed the list off, and Mom stuck it front and centre on the fridge door, so there'll be no excuses for failing to follow through.

1. NO ELECTRONIC DEVICES AT THE KITCHEN TABLE
2. ONE HOUR OF NON-LINE (my word) ACTIVITY AFTER DINNER EACH EVENING, SUCH AS GOING FOR A WALK, READING A BOOK, PLAYING A GAME, ETC.
3. REGULAR FAMILY MOVIE NIGHTS
4. NO TEXTING ANYONE INSIDE THE HOUSE
5. LOW-TECH SUNDAYS
6. BEFORE BED, DEVICES MUST BE LEFT IN THE KITCHEN, TURNED OFF

That afternoon, we all played Monopoly and had a blast. Then we watched a Will Ferrell comedy after supper and laughed together as a family for the first time in ages. Even Zach didn't seem so mad any more, especially after Mom found an easy recipe online (*that* was allowed) for savoury cheese and garlic popcorn, and he helped her make it.

My favourite rule is #6. It's also the one that I came up with. And the one Zach isn't crazy about. I like it because it means I won't have my phone in my hand until after breakfast each morning.

Dad and Mom like the idea, too. They even dug out their old clock radio and set it to wake up to classical music each day. Dad got his old watch out from his sock drawer and displayed it proudly on his wrist. It was a gift from us kids one Father's Day, when we were toddlers (which our mom had bought and wrapped up for us). He used to wear it constantly, until he became permanently glued to his phone and tablet.

"Just like in the good old days," Dad told us with a wry smile. "Before we relied on our smartphones for absolutely everything. Before they replaced our brains."

Mom found a vintage alarm clock in a cupboard, which she'd picked up at Value Village. One you actually have to wind. I snatched that one up pretty quick. It has a cool cartoon cat on it, and the cat's eyes and tail move back and forth as each second ticks by. The alarm is jarring, but why not try waking up the way people used to back in the olden days? Zach seemed a bit jealous until he heard the alarm jangle. Then he decided it would be okay for Dad to wake him each morning until he gets an alarm clock of his own.

The one thing we decided we could use our smartphones for on Sundays was actual phone calls. Dad said that since we no longer have a landline, we need to have a phone available in case someone wants to reach us. And, after much discussion, we all agreed that speaking to friends on low-tech day is okay, as long as we don't spend all day yapping, or cheat and text while our phones are switched on.

That means I'm not breaking any rules when I use my phone later that evening to make a phone call. Or to attempt to make a phone call. I really want to talk to Jake, to apologize for giving him a hard time about Spencer. And ask him to the Sadie Hawkins dance, which is next Saturday.

He probably already has a date, which wouldn't be the worst thing. I mean, would we even be able to talk like we used to? Our lives are so different now.

I hit his number at least five times, but I cancel each call before it rings, so my name won't show up. How lame. Did I really think I'd magically morph into someone daring enough to ask out the hottest guy in grade ten?

Oh well, there's always tomorrow. And what a relief it is going to bed without my phone right beside me. Instead, I open a fantasy novel, one I've been meaning to read for a long time. And I actually read a whole chapter before my eyes slam shut.

5

"WHAT IS YOUR *problem*, Clemen*tine*? I tried to reach you all afternoon yesterday? Didn't you get my texts or phone messages?"

That's the very first thing my "friend" Ellie says to me at my locker on Monday morning. And I cannot *wait* to break the news to her.

"I never even got your messages until this morning. But I didn't reply because I knew I'd see you first thing at school. My phone was off almost all day yesterday."

Ellie gapes at me as if she thinks I've totally lost my mind.

"What are you, *nuts*?"

I shrug. "New family rules. Our folks decided we all have to start limiting our online time. That means shutting off our phones way more often, and not randomly surfing the net, or checking for messages and posts every few minutes."

"Huh? And you're *okay* with that? You're not freaking out? It's practically prehistoric!"

"Don't have much choice. We're all doing it. We kind of made a family pact."

"That's the weirdest thing I ever heard," she says, frowning. "What do you even find to do at home, anyway?"

"You'd be surprised. Yesterday we played a board game then watched a movie together. It was fun. Honest. And in the evenings we have to do stuff like that for at least an hour."

Ellie's face sags. "Wow. So whose dumbass idea was that anyway? Your mom's or your dad's?"

Mine, I want to holler. "Can't even remember now."

Ellie's dark eyes look suspicious. She shifts her backpack from one shoulder to the other, then glances around as if she's looking for someone to share my crazy story with. But, of course, it's hard to get anyone's attention in the halls because of where everyone's eyes are always focused. It's a wonder we don't all have some sort of permanent neck injuries from non-stop texting. A few seconds later the bell rings, and as I turn to head for my first class of the day, Ellie grabs my sleeve.

"Wait a sec, Clems. I really need to talk to you about next weekend. Something major is happening with me and Mac, and I need your help remember? Meet me here after first period. It's really important."

I yank my arm loose. "Later, Ellie. Gotta get all the way across the school to science lab. Dissecting worms today!" Then I bolt before she can try to stop me.

SOMEHOW OR OTHER I find a way to avoid Ellie for the rest of the morning, but that doesn't stop her from texting me every hour.

Clems where r u? Why didn't you meet me? I need u.
Clementine why r u avoiding me?

Hey Clem is something wrong?

Answer me, willya, OMG what is up with u?

And every time I give her the same reply: Sorry, major busy right now.

I make myself scarce at lunchtime by ducking into study hall to work on an English essay. How pathetic to hide from one of my oldest friends because I'm afraid of what she might ask me to do next. I so do *not* want a replay of her mom showing up at our door, totally pissed off. I'm sick having to lie for her over and over again, all because of the secret she's holding against me.

Before last period, I stop by my locker to grab my coat and stuff. As soon as the bell rings, I bolt out the front doors into the crisp October air, feeling smug. With careful planning, I've managed to avoid running into Ellie for the entire day. Only a few kids have spilled out of the school before me. I set off walking, trying to keep the hunger rumbles at bay as I head for the plaza to buy a bag of chips.

Suddenly I hear a different kind of rumble from behind me: skateboard wheels on the road.

When I turn around, Jake is zooming up, both hands texting on his phone, earbuds plugged into his head. He's multi-tasking big time and completely oblivious to the busy intersection he's approaching, where I'm also headed to cross the street. This is a four-way, so cars have to stop in every direction before proceeding on through. I can already tell that Jake is definitely not stopping, because he doesn't have a clue where he is. Which is why I do what I need to do.

I whip my backpack off my shoulder and fling it straight at him. I hear the *oomph* when it hits him in the belly and knocks him off his skateboard. He drops his phone as he lands hard on the boulevard a metre away from me. His empty skateboard rolls on through the intersection and instantly gets struck by a passing car. Another car pulls up to the curb to make sure he's okay, but I wave the driver on.

Jake sits on the grass looking totally dazed. One earbud dangles now, the other still jammed in his ear.

"What the hell just happened?" He reaches for his phone, which is protected with a heavy-duty rubber case, probably in case of dumb wipeouts like this one. Then he scrambles to his feet and shakes his head a couple of times like he's trying to reboot his brain.

"I think I just saved your life," I tell him. "Didn't mean to hit you so hard, but I have a ton of homework tonight. Sorry about that. You should really watch where you're going."

Then I scoop up my fully loaded backpack and walk away. My entire body is vibrating like mad. I think my teeth may even be chattering.

"Hey, hang on for a sec, would ya, Clem?" he calls behind me. "Let me grab my skateboard, okay."

There's a huge crack right down the middle, but the wheels, I figure, are probably worth salvaging, from what little I know of these things. Jake walks up to me shaking his head again like he still can't quite understand what just happened.

"Can you believe it? I just bought this deck, like, a week ago."

"You should be happy you didn't crack your *head*, shouldn't you? I'm thinking *helmet*." I totally exaggerate an eye roll. "Boys and their toys."

Jake's face drops, then he grins. "Hmm, you got a point, even though you sound like my mom. Seriously, thanks, Clem. I owe you one for this. I had no clue what hit me."

"That could have turned out way worse." I frown because he doesn't seem nearly as shocked about this as I am. Then again, he's probably used to this stuff.

"Yep, you're right. Extremely dumb. My parents warn me every time someone gets hit by a car while they're walking and texting at the same time. Hey, looks like we're heading in the same direction."

He starts loping along in step beside me, and my heart threatens to launch right out of my mouth. *Looks like now's my chance.* But I can't get past what happened on Saturday morning, when he was pissed at me after we talked about Spencer. Maybe he's over it since I just saved his life. But that almost makes it worse. If I ask him to the dance now, he'll have to say yes because he'll figure he owes me. Suddenly, I want to kick something hard — I'm that mad.

"Look, Jake," I say, since neither of us have said anything for a couple of seconds. "I'm sorry about that stuff I said on Saturday. I guess everything about Kit is still really bugging me, so I spoke up about Spencer."

Jake stops dead. For a second I'm afraid he's about to take off again. Then he looks me straight in the eye.

"I'm sorry I snapped," he says. "But Spence is freaking out after what Ms. Stitski said at the assembly. He knows damn well she meant him when she said those things about being cruel and stuff. It's like she wants him to take the fall. He had nothing to do with it, though. No matter what anyone wants to believe. And I'd *swear* to that."

"Okay," I murmur. I can't even look at him because of what's gnawing away at my conscience.

"But, guess what? I actually left the plaza right after you did on Saturday. Right before the cops showed up. So you're kind of like my lucky charm." His smile is so sweet I can practically taste it on my tongue.

"Well, that's cool, I guess," I tell him. *Extremely* cool. Jake actually listened to me and understood that I was genuinely concerned! *Ask him to the* dance! *Right now, stupid!* Except "I'm stopping off at the plaza," comes out, instead. *Idiot!*

"Sounds like a plan. I'm in. Need a Gatorade. Hey, let me at least treat you for saving my life, okay? Anything you want."

"A bag of chips and a Coke," I tell him.

"That's *it*?" He grins and I melt a little. "That means I still owe you."

"No you *don't*," I insist as we push our way into the convenience store. "Anyone would have done the same thing. You think I was just gonna let you die?" *The way I did with Kit?*

Jake looks at me funny, and his face changes ever so slightly. I'm sure mine has, too. Why did I even say that? What a dumbass line after what happened with Kit.

Jake looks like he's about to say something, but then he heads down the aisle for the drinks. I scan the bags of chips. Hmm, new flavour on the shelf. Chicken and gravy? Never tried that one. Just as I reach for the bag, Jake comes pushing past me. He hands me a Coke and five bucks. His face is stiff, his eyes shifty.

"I just remembered. I'm supposed to be somewhere, and I'm late already." Then he's gone like a shot out the door.

"Huh, that's weird," I say to the clerk who's staring at the empty doorway. "Guess he wasn't as thirsty as he thought. He's treating me. Which is why he gave me the five bucks." I hand over the money, wondering why I felt the need to explain Jake's strange behaviour.

From the corner of my eye, I spot someone striding up the aisle from the cooler section. She's holding a milk jug, and she has her hand on a kid's shoulder. She's dressed smartly in a tailored, grey suit, but her face looks worn, used up. My insides turn to mush. Kit Stitski's mom and brother. I grab the chips and pop from the counter.

"Keep the change," I say, then dash out the door without even looking back.

MY HUNGER RUMBLES have turned into something like nausea. As I walk home, I can't even break into the bag of chips. The instant I laid eyes on Kit's mom and his little brother, Kevin, everything awful that happened four months ago came spinning at me like a rogue tornado. Yet again.

In the news reports, it said that Ms. Stitski didn't even realize Kit was missing from his bedroom until she went to wake him the next morning. The last time she checked on him, he was playing an online game in his room. At some point after that, he'd left their huge home on the outskirts of town. Everyone's theory was that he saw something about the party on social media and he left his house.

The news also said that the police were asking for witnesses. They wanted to talk with anyone who'd seen

Kit at the field party, so they could try and track his final steps. His mom came forward as well, to speak to the media and make an emotional plea on TV.

Just like at the assembly on Friday, she begged for somebody to give the authorities something to work with. There had to have been over a hundred kids at that party, maybe even one-fifty (it's not like anyone bothered to count). But in the end, maybe ten kids stepped up to tell the cops they'd seen Kit that night. Nobody said they'd seen him leave though.

The coroner's inquest called it "death by misadventure." Kit Stitski had wandered away from the party, slipped off the edge of the quarry, and drowned. Everyone knew that Ms. Stitski wasn't thrilled with the verdict. But she had such an intimidating way of voicing her opinions, it was sure to send any potential witnesses scurrying like scared mice. Who'd want to face the wrath of Joan Stitski, the angry mother bear looking for retribution? I'd certainly kept my distance from her. What if she could tell I knew something?

Because of that, I never went to Kit's funeral. I told my parents I was too upset, which wasn't exactly a lie. And I just hung out in my room that day thinking about Kit, while my folks went to a family funeral out of town. But if it were a lie, it wouldn't have been the first one I'd told them about that night. I was ashamed too, for not having the guts to step forward and tell the police what I knew. And now I can't even live with myself anymore.

MONDAY EVENING I can't concentrate on school work. I can't stop thinking about Jake, and what triggered his bizarre reaction in the convenience store. One minute we were hanging out together, and the next he was gone, totally ditching me there with the so-sad Stitskis.

He looked as if he'd seen a ghost just before bolting. And maybe he had, the same as me when I saw Kit's heartsick mother and brother. Was Jake haunted by his memories of Kit like I was? Like the Stitskis obviously were? Much like Banquo's ghost from *Macbeth*, Kit has become a "horrible shadow" on all our lives.

As I hunch over my English essay after dinner, it's almost as though Kit is right there at my elbow.

"Quit my sight. Let the earth hide thee," I murmur to my empty room, and shiver. That line from Shakespeare got stuck in my head the instant I read the play in theatre arts this year.

Guilt is haunting me just like it was Macbeth. No wonder I can't stop thinking about that spooky scene. And if I wasn't crazy about Shakespeare's plays before, now I'm beginning to despise them.

Ms. Raven, our drama teacher, told us that it's bad luck for actors to say *Macbeth* in a theatre during a production. Apparently, the play was eternally cursed after an actor died during the original production, when a real dagger was used instead of the prop.

Nowadays, actors have to call it "the Scottish play," and if they mess up and say the word *Macbeth*, they have to spit over their shoulder or run around the theatre three times and recite a line from Shakespeare. Weird, but fascinating. We all listened, rapt, to her spooky stories about the play's performances centuries ago. I suppose those tales hit home even more for me since I happen to have a ghost of my own.

I can practically hear Kit whispering in my ear. *"What time is it, Clementine?"* He said the same thing to me almost every day in middle school. Sometimes it drove me nuts, but I always told him the time because it seemed to make him so happy. He stopped saying it in grade nine, though. I guess it's because I hardly ever ran into him anymore. Until the night of the party, just before he disappeared, when he said it for the very last time. Now I'd give anything just to have him ask me again.

As soon as I turn my phone on after non-line time, the texts start flying.

R u ignoring me Clems?

Srsly what is ur problem?

I ignore those two, hoping she'll give up and go away. I answer a few texts from some of my other friends, but Ellie keeps on trying.

I know ur txting every1 else.

Sorry Els, missed ur txts. Sup? I definitely do *not* want to know what's up.

Can u cover for me this wknd?

Ur mom is on 2 u, u know, I text back. U can't keep lying to her. Me neither.

U don't understand ☹ this is majorly IMPORTANT. It always is!!!!!!!!!!!!!!!!!!

Clems, I'm helping YOU. By NOT telling. Help me plz!

Again, I want to pitch my phone at the wall or flush it down the toilet. Hmm. Maybe that would work. People drop their phones into toilets by accident all the time.

But I'm sick of trying to find excuses. I need to find a way to get rid of this Ellie problem once and for all. And I guess there is one. But I still don't think I can come clean to my parents. Or face Ms. Stitski.

Tell me what u need at school tmrrw, I text back.

Then I shut my phone off for the rest of the evening and head to the family room to watch *Big Bang Theory* reruns with my family.

Ellie makes it easy to unplug from my phone. I'm totally loving this new house rule!

6

I DREAD MEETING up with Ellie this morning, but it has to happen eventually. She's in my theatre arts class, and that's on today's schedule. I head there after announcements.

The rest of our classmates are already trickling into the auditorium by the time I arrive, some through the shadowy wings, and others up the main aisle. I love everything about theatre arts, but the best part is how we get to be anyone we want to in this class, as encouraged by our teacher, Ms. Raven. Ellie is already waiting for me, sitting on the apron of the stage with her long legs dangling. As soon as she spots me, she waves me right over, and I go, feeling a bit like a well-trained dog. She only has to snap her fingers or whistle, and there I am, wagging my tail, or at least pretending to.

"Hey, Els." My lips feel too tight to form a smile.

"God, you're hard to reach." She tilts her head. "I didn't see you for the rest of yesterday, and you didn't even meet me after school."

"Wow, I totally forgot. Way too much on my mind. There's this essay that —"

But she cuts me off and just starts blabbering. "Okay, so this weekend. Mac is going to party with his university friends. He's staying in their residence, and he wants *me* to come! Can you freakin' believe it? *Me* hanging out with university kids! Sick!"

"What's that got to do with me?" I feel sick right down to my toes.

"So, I came up with this plan. And trust me, it's great. It'll work. Okay, so, on Friday night I get my mom to drop me off at your place for the weekend. I'll tell her we have to work on a project with a bunch of other kids or something. Then I'll tell her we're all going to the Sadie Hawkins dance on Saturday night, too. And I'll actually stay over with you on Friday night."

I hate the sound of her plan already. "What if I'm busy Friday night?"

It's like I haven't even spoken. Her eyes are weird and bright, and she's gesturing madly, as though she's directing an orchestra. I spot some marks on her upper arm and think of a banana for some reason. Then I remember how her mom grabbed her and yanked her through the door the other day. Did she do that? It's hard to believe, but she really was pissed at her.

"Saturday morning Mac will pick me up, and we'll head over to party at the university for the night. He'll drop me off at your place before noon on Sunday, and my mom can pick me up there. I'll stay in touch with her all weekend: I'll tell her how our project is coming along and how fun the dance is. She won't even suspect that I'm not with you."

Ellie takes a deep breath then sits there with this wide, rapturous smile, as though she's just come up with a solution to end world hunger.

"Are you out of your *mind*? You'll never get away with it."

"Not if you don't help me." Her smile dissolves, her dark eyes narrow. "You *will* help me, won't you? Because if you don't …"

When a hand lands hard on my shoulder, I jump, and so does Ellie. I look up. Aubrey is standing on the stage, leaning over us.

"*When shall we three meet again?*" she says in a dramatic, witchy voice as she wraps an arm around each of our shoulders.

"*In thunder, lightning, or in rain?*" I croak back at her.

Ellie's nose wrinkles as her face turns sour. "You really are a witch, Aubrey. With a capital B." She jumps from the stage and glares at us before walking off to pout in one of the auditorium seats. Saved by *Macbeth*'s witches, act I, scene 1. For now, anyway.

"Wow. Sorry, did I interrupt something?" Aubrey sits beside me on the edge of the stage. "Because, seriously, Ellie's face looks like she just stepped in dog crap." Aubrey adjusts her paisley bandana. How I envy those wispy curls that spring from her head in every direction. My own hair is flat-iron straight, all the time.

"Nope, we were done," I say, grinning for probably the first time that day. I almost feel like hugging her for coming to my rescue.

Ellie isn't thrilled about my relationship with Aubrey. She feels threatened or something because the more time I spend with Aubrey, the less I have to devote to her.

The very best thing about this new friend of mine is that she *wasn't* at the quarry that night. She will never be part of the plot, because she'll never have a clue what really happened.

When I'm around Aubrey, I can almost feel close to normal, close to the carefree way I used to feel all the time. And even though she's loud and can be a bit goofy sometimes, Aubrey can always find a way to make me smile.

Which is more than I can say about Ellie.

WHEN I STOP by my locker to grab my lunch, Jake is loitering nearby. Just randomly leaning against the wall by the lockers, trying to look casual as he chews on a fingernail. It's a dead giveaway. Our eyes meet, and he raises his brows, trying to look cool or surprised or something.

"Oh, hey, Clem, I didn't know your locker was here."

"Well, now you do," I tell him as I spin my combination lock, and my heart thumps right up into my throat. "So, are you holding up the wall or waiting for a bus or what?"

Jake grins. "You crack me up. You always say exactly what you're thinking, don't you? There's just no pretending with you."

"Depends on the circumstances," I say with my head shoved inside my locker, so he won't see me blushing. I crouch over and pretend to rifle around for something until the burning stops. He has no idea how good I am at pretending.

"Okay, so you figured it out." From the corner of my eye, I can see him coming closer. "I was actually looking for you just now. I asked someone where your locker is. Because I need to talk to you. About what happened yesterday. In the store."

I jerk up and bash my forehead on my locker shelf. I stand there rubbing the sore spot. And I thought it was hard to look at him before.

"Ouch," he says, closer still. "That's *gotta* hurt."

"So, what *about* the store?" I say to my reflection in my locker mirror. Hopefully not too bad of a bump, but I look half-stunned. *Ugh.*

"Sorry I bounced like that." He's right beside me now, speaking in a low voice as if he wants to be sure nobody else will hear. The halls are always packed with kids just before lunch period, but it almost feels like we're the only ones there.

"You lied about needing to be somewhere yesterday, didn't you?" I say. "And totally ditched me. *With them.*"

Now I can see his grim face beside mine in the mirror. His nostrils flare slightly, and his blue eyes are blinking way too fast, like he's having trouble keeping it together. He rubs them with the heel of his hand and sighs. "Okay, so you figured that out. What else, Clem? Are you thinking of going to Ms. Stitski to tell her you know something? If Spencer's name comes up again, she'll be sold on it."

I am totally speechless for a moment. He turns to walk away. No way am I letting him go this time. I grab the back of his T-shirt, and he turns around.

"God, Jake, is that what you *really* think? That I'd rat Spencer out? Why would I do that?"

He twists free of my grip. "I don't even know what the hell to think anymore," he says in a dismal voice. "Because I don't trust *anybody*. Kit's mom is out to get someone, and it could be any of us if somebody says the wrong thing to the cops." He scrubs his face again. "It's making me crazy!"

"Me, too," I confess. "You know what? I threw your five bucks at the clerk and ran out of the store yesterday, too. Bolted just like you did." I think for a second. If Jake's afraid to talk to the cops about the quarry party, then maybe we have more in common than I thought. I take a chance. "How about we go find some place to talk, Jake?"

"I was hoping you'd say that," he says.

WE HEAD FOR the music room, a space not much bigger than a storage closet, where the piano and all the music stands and stools are stored. It's right beside the auditorium, and nobody ever goes in there unless we're setting up for a play or concert.

We sit on stools facing the wall instead of each other. I unpack my lunch, a tuna sandwich that I made this morning, and a juice box. Jake bought a chicken wrap and pop in the cafeteria. We eat quietly for a few minutes. Should I risk it and speak first? In the muffled closeness of the room, Kit's ghost seems to drift like bonfire smoke over our heads.

Jake sucks in a deep breath. "I couldn't even go to the funeral."

"Me neither," I admit. "I still can't face his family."

"Okay, so I really need to get this off my chest, Clem. But please don't breathe a word to anyone, okay?" A long and suffocating pause. "I think Kit died because of me."

7

I CAN'T EVEN speak. I can't believe he just said what I was about to say myself. If I'd taken the chance and spoken first, Jake would have heard identical words: *I think Kit died because of me.*

"Why would you ever think that?" I manage to choke out through a mouthful of sandwich.

Another long pause as Jake slowly chews and stares into space.

"He was there because of me," he finally says.

My sandwich is squashed in my hand now. "Come on. You can't blame yourself for him being there. Word got out way too fast. Everyone was going on about it."

Jake looks at me sideways with a sickly smile.

"Yeah, but he actually went *with* me. I ran into him. Right near his house. He told me where he was going and asked if we could walk together." Jake crumples his food wrapper into a tight ball and pitches it into a trash can. "And you know, for a second I thought maybe I should just take him home. That maybe it *wasn't* such a great idea for him to be at the quarry that night. But then I thought, what the hell? Kit deserves to have fun sometimes. He shouldn't have to miss out on so much stuff just 'cause he's challenged."

"I know what you mean. I always felt sorry for him back in middle school because he couldn't do the same things as the rest of us. But, god, remember how he danced *non-stop* with *everyone* at dance-a-thons? He loved parties. He loved to do what everyone else was doing."

"He cracked me up whenever he tried out my skateboard. He'd sort of tip over sideways in slow motion. He was a really cool kid."

"I was in a couple of school plays with him. He learned his lines, and everyone else's, like a champ, but he was totally unpredictable. Sometimes he'd just wander onstage in the middle of a scene, and the audience would laugh because it was so sweet." I can't help but laugh a little just reminiscing. Then I feel guilty for it.

"And that thing with the watches, how he sometimes wore three at once. He'd always check your wrist to see if you were wearing one." Jake grins and shakes his head. "I heard everyone wore a watch to his funeral."

"Yeah, I heard that, too. Remember how sometimes kids would even give him their old watches? And how he was obsessed with the weather? He always gave a daily weather report during morning announcements. He sounded just like a real radio announcer."

We actually smile at each other, just recalling our memories of Kit.

"Clem, I honestly planned to keep an eye on him that night, and I did most of the time, but then he disappeared." Jake's voice is huskier now. "I thought he just went home. And like a total loser, I didn't even check. Because I was having too much fun partying."

And I was having a crap time watching you party and wishing you'd notice me.

"So, what's the deal with Spencer?" I say instead. "What's freaking him out so much? And why are you working so hard to protect him?"

Jake slumps forward, elbows on his knees, chin on his hands. He stares at the wall. "Spencer did it again that night. Gave Kit a hard time, trying to impress some girls, make them laugh or something. Now it's blowing up in his face. You were there. You saw what happened, right?"

My nod is a lie. I saw a commotion in the shadows near the fire. I didn't see what caused it. I didn't see how it ended. I didn't see anything else but Jake. All I heard were the rumours afterward that started over the summer, about Spencer bullying Kit. About some sort of scuffle.

"That stupid rumour about a fight started spreading, and it turned into something way worse than it actually was. Spencer's scared Ms. Stitski thinks it went further than it actually did, because she's never heard the real version of the story. But Kit didn't even get upset after Spencer tripped him. Remember? He just sat on the ground and laughed. And then some kids helped him get up."

Oh, god. Spencer is sitting on his own prickly secret.

"And I pulled Spencer aside and bitched him out after it happened. I told him that Kit came to the party with me and I was looking out for him."

"God, Jake," I whisper. "I never even knew that."

"There was no way I could step forward and tell the cops that, because I was scared to get questioned even more, maybe even blamed for everything else that went wrong that night. For letting him follow me there in the first place, then not taking care of him." He gulps hard.

"So you're covering each other's butts?"

"Pretty much. Some other kids were nearby that night and saw what Spencer did. A couple even told the cops that a fight never happened, but what if the cops don't believe it? And what if someone decides to throw his name out there to Ms. Stitski again, when she already has him on her radar screen? He needs all the backup he can get right now. So do I. And he knows that Kit followed me there. He's the only one who knows, besides you now. So I have to help him out, right?"

"You mean he's making sure you help him out by getting you to kill all the stupid rumours?"

Jake nods slowly. "That's right, and I'm doing my best. But the thing is, right after those kids helped Kit up, he took off toward the bushes. The rest of us went on partying. Didn't follow him or watch out for him. And I just can't forgive myself for that." A tear glints in the corner of his eye. He looks away.

I cram the rest of my sandwich back into my lunch bag. Jake has no clue that while he was partying, I was watching *him*. As he whooped and hollered around the fire, dancing like crazy to the blasting music, I'd followed his every move.

There's no way I'm going to tell him that. That I'd danced alone in the shadows, watching and waiting and hoping that maybe he'd notice me, maybe even talk to me — but way too nervous to make a move myself. The pretty girls who lusted after him were lurking nearby that night, too, flirting madly, and I knew I didn't stand a chance. But it didn't stop my pathetic, sappy longing.

I should be crazy happy now that Jake is sitting right beside me. Instead, though, something like a quiet calm has settled over me. Maybe this is a good thing. He may not be a potential boyfriend, or even a date for the Sadie Hawkins, but maybe I've found myself a companion in misery.

But, I can't let him go on believing that the whole thing is his fault.

"Well, guess what, Jake? It wasn't your fault, or Spencer's. It was mine. Because, actually, *I* was the last one to see him alive that night."

Jake spins on his stool and stares straight at me. "What are you talking about?"

I don't look away, don't even blink. It's my turn to share a secret.

"I'm pretty sure that right after Kit went toward the bushes, he practically ran right into me. And you know what? It gets even worse."

Then I tell him what nobody else but Ellie knows. About how Kit needed to find a place to pee in private that night, and I'd sent him into the bushes. How I was probably the very last person to see him, but just like Jake, I hadn't gone looking for him.

Jake's face changes as he listens to my version of that night, as if a light is growing brighter behind his eyes. I explain how I kept my mouth shut when the police were asking questions and looking for witnesses, because I didn't want my own truth to come out. There were so many people who would be disappointed in me, and who might stop trusting me because I took my eyes off Kit. And then there was Ms. Stitski, the pitbull lawyer. I couldn't take that risk. Jake nods and admits that's exactly why he did the same dumbass thing. It's almost as if we're partners in a crime we didn't really commit.

We stare at each other for a few seconds, trying to take it all in, I guess. For the first time in months I don't feel so alone.

"So, now what?" I ask. "It's almost like we opened up Pandora's box, isn't it? All this horrible stuff is flying out, and there's no way to put it back."

"Well, I don't know about you, but I feel better now that's all out in the open, at least between us, even though it doesn't kill the guilt. And from what I remember about the Pandora myth, there was Hope in the box, too, right?"

"Huh, that's true." And then I think of something that hadn't hit me before. "But what if someone *else* really did see something and isn't saying, just like us?"

"But the inquest ruled it was death by misadventure," Jake reminds me.

"Maybe that's what they had to say. Maybe since nobody offered them any solid leads, and because of the lack of evidence, the investigation had to end there. But what if there is more to it than that? What if something happened to Kit after he met up with me?"

"Oh, come on, Clem." Jake seems to force a chuckle. "That's a bit of a stretch. Kit got lost in the dark and slipped into the quarry, just like they said. Makes perfect sense, doesn't it?"

"Maybe. But maybe not. Because if we couldn't talk about it 'til now, Jake …"

He reaches out and touches my hand. "Then who else still can't talk about it. And why?"

I squeeze his hand. "Right. Did they hurt Kit, or are they just afraid, like us? Because I sure don't want to take the fall for someone else."

Jake thinks for a moment. "That's right, Clem. If someone else comes forward about Kit, our names might come up. Like, what if Spencer gets scared and decides to tell Ms. Stitski about my part in getting Kit there?" Jake looks sick again. "She's a lawyer. She's obviously great at building cases. Criminal negligence causing death. Isn't that an actual offence? And even if I didn't commit a crime, I showed a total lack of responsibility. I'll look like a complete asshole to everyone in town. God, I'll never even be able to get a job or anything. Who would ever want to trust me?"

"Me too, Jake," I murmur.

We both sit perfectly still in the hush of the music room, the concrete walls and closed door muffling the din of an ordinary school day. It feels safe here, especially now that all the raw nastiness we've been concealing has finally been exposed to somebody we can trust. Each other.

"So, what should we do?" I whisper, as my heart flutters with a new understanding that we have to try and do something. We can't just let this thing go.

"I have no clue," Jake tells me. "It was almost easier just hanging on to everything."

"That's true. But you know what I think we should do first?"

Jake shakes his head, though he seems afraid. "What?"

"We should go over and visit Ms. Stitski. Tell her how sorry we are for skipping out on everything back in June. And maybe we can find out what she's looking for, how much she already knows. See if she actually believes the rumours. Or has any other clues about what happened that night."

Jake sighs. "I was hoping you wouldn't say that."

AT DINNER MY thoughts are stuck in an endless loop, going over the plans we made about paying a visit to the Stitskis this week. It was my brilliant idea, but I've already begun to regret it. I'm still not sure that I'm ready to face Kit's broken family. Or that I ever will be.

Since deciding to log off, it feels like a chore to make small talk at meal times, but we've been trying hard during the few meals we've shared since my *other* brilliant idea in the restaurant on Sunday. We chat about things that are going on in our country and in the world, and we share ideas and listen to each other's thoughts and opinions. Now we actually have to try to think for a change, instead of relying on our smartphones to think for us.

Mom seems to be suffering the most without her device on hand all the time. After two days with the new rules, she isn't adapting very well. It's kind of pathetic and kind of funny to watch how her eyes stray toward her phone, sitting switched off with the others on the kitchen desk. A couple of times I've caught her making unconscious swiping motions on the table with her fingertip, as though it was her phone screen.

And I thought *I* was hooked.

"Don't worry, Mom," I said when I noticed her checking out her phone last night. "I'm sure you're not missing anything momentous on Twitter." Caught, she shot me a scathing look through narrowed eyes.

This time though, lost in my own muddled thoughts, I'm not paying attention to anything. And since nobody has a device beside their plate to focus on, everybody else notices *me*.

"You don't have much to say today," Dad says.

"Huh?" I look up from my plate of spaghetti, mid-twirl. Three sets of eyes are on me.

"Well, usually you're the one who has the most to say, Clems." He pats my hand across the table. "Yesterday you talked about your theatre arts class, and the skits based on *Macbeth* that you had to ad lib, and how funny it was. Then you shocked us with the big reveal that you have a soft spot for spiders and would never kill one since they eat the nastier bugs. But today you don't even seem to be at the table with us."

"Probably thinking about Jake," Zach says though a mouthful of meatball. He winces when I boot him under the table.

Dad has a worried look on his face, which is strange to see. Then I realize it's because I hardly ever get to see his face this way. Usually it's focused on a screen instead of on me, even when he talks to me. So I'd better engage instead of ignore.

"Yeah, you're right," I tell him. "The truth is, Kit Stitski's been on my mind lately."

Surprised faces all around the table. Then a solemn look from Mom.

"Funny you should mention that, Clems. Kit's name came up at my school today because of his brother, Kevin, who's in grade five. We actually had a staff meeting about him." She taps one finger on the table and shakes her head. "You know, I still feel so badly that nobody from our family was able to make it to Kit's funeral. It was just sad luck that Dad and I had to go to his great-aunt's funeral out of town on the same day."

"And me too, remember?" Zach says, pulling a face. "It was so frigging boring!"

"Jeez, Zach," Dad tells him, frowning. "She was my Godmother!"

"Yeah, sad luck," I say with a sigh. "So what was the staff meeting about anyway?" I ask, curious now.

"That's so sad too, Clem. Kevin's been acting up this year, and that's not like him. He was in my class last year, and an excellent student. Always respectful, homework and projects done on time, pretty good grades. But all that has changed, and we're getting concerned now."

"Clearly, missing his brother," Dad says, nodding in an understanding way. "And who can blame him? So what are they doing about it?"

"Well, there's talk of bringing in a social worker and getting him some counselling. We'd like to get together with Kevin and his mom, but she's a tough one to get hold of. Extremely busy lawyer, I suppose, and when she actually answers her phone, she says she'll call us back but never does. A lot of the time Kevin doesn't show up at school. He used to be such a bright, happy kid, too. It's a real shame. I wish I knew of a way to help him."

I feel even sicker just hearing that about Kevin. "It's still pretty fresh, Mom. If I'm still thinking about Kit, then a lot of other people must be, too, *especially* his brother. It's like nobody wants to talk about him, and even for me there was never any real closure."

"No closure, Clementine?" Mom looks at me funny. "But you went to the school after he died, and spoke with the counsellor, didn't you, and took part in the special activities? And you went to the memorial at the quarry, right?"

Nope. Wrong. "Whatever, Mom. I don't feel like talking about it anymore."

I suck up a long strand of spaghetti, knowing that she's still watching me. I've never admitted that I didn't go, *couldn't go*, to that evening vigil that the Circle of Friends and a bunch of other kids had pulled together on a whim at the quarry, the day they found him there. That I just went for a long bike ride alone instead and texted my friends that I was sick. At the time I felt so lame missing out that I had to make something up. I pretended I'd gone, telling my folks what everyone else told me. How everyone gathered at the quarry, and lit candles and said prayers. How all the kids wore watches to the vigil and a few of them read poems. Then someone had brought out a guitar, and everyone joined in singing one of Kit's favourite songs, Great Big Sea's "Ordinary Day."

No doubt about it, and no use denying it: my life has become a big, fat lie since Kit died. I just sit there staring at my plate for a few minutes, afraid of looking up, knowing that all eyes in the room are on me. Then finally I can't take it anymore.

I smile weakly and shrug, then put my half-empty plate on the counter and head for my room. Yet another half-eaten meal because of my messed-up life.

How weird that ever since my family's disconnected, we seem more connected than ever.

8

ON WEDNESDAY MORNING, Ellie isn't at my locker. I haven't heard a word from her since theatre arts yesterday, when she pouted after Aubrey surprised us on stage. She hasn't even texted, which is strange considering how much she usually pesters me.

Something else about Ellie has been bothering me since I opened my eyes this morning. Yesterday Jake and I decided that some of the other kids from the field party have to know more, but they aren't talking either. Jake and I couldn't have been the only ones who ran into Kit that night. There were kids everywhere. Over a hundred of them. What *else* did they see? As we walked home together after school, plotting our visit to the Stitskis this week, we also concluded that it's time to start asking other kids questions, to try and learn more about what actually happened to Kit. *After* he crossed paths with the two of us.

Ever since "it" happened, Ellie has held it over me, threatening to expose me. But the fact is, she hasn't breathed a word to me about what she saw that night. And now that I know Jake was hiding a secret, I'm very curious about Ellie too. Because what better way for her to hang on to her own secrets than to threaten to blab mine if I don't agree to her selfish demands? It's totally evil, and it's also a perfect plan. And I have a sick feeling now that I've been totally sucked in.

She's definitely the first person I'm going to question.

When Jake shows up at my locker, though, my Ellie fixation is history in a matter of seconds. I can hardly believe what just the sound of his voice can do to me now — like make my insides bubble and boil like a lab experiment. What it would be like to actually kiss this guy?

"I slept like crap," is the first thing he says. "Yesterday's stuff kept waking me up."

"Me, too. It's like the whole thing is fresh again. I'm already dreading what we decided. How'll we ever face his family?"

"Don't worry. We'll get through this together, Clems." He rubs the back of his hand against my arm, takes a step closer to me as his blue eyes settle on mine and —

The first-period bell buzzes right over our heads.

"Catch you later," he says, and strides off down the hall.

ELLIE'S FIRST TEXT of the day comes at the end of first period. Her words are waiting to annoy me the instant I switch on my phone.

Clems! Meet me in the w/room right now! Plzzz!

Don't want to be late for history, I text back.

THIS IS IMPORTANT!!!! HURRY!!!!

So are my marks.

I NEED u! Just for a minute.

And that's all the time I'm giving you. Of course I don't say that, but I don't text back, either. Instead, I let her worry about me *not* rushing to her rescue, as I rush through the hallways to her rescue. Again. This time I have an ulterior motive, though. I have some questions to ask. And only a couple of minutes to ask them before the next bell.

A couple of giggling girls, drenched in body spray, shuffle out of the washroom door just as I reach it, and I step aside to let them pass. What can possibly be worth giggling about, or stinking for, this early in the day? As the creaky door swings shut behind me, the sound echoes off the walls. Nobody's in there. One stall door is shut, probably because the toilet is clogged up with paper or *worse*. As usual.

"Dammit!" I say out loud. She's not even here.

"Clems?" Her voice makes me jump.

"Where *are* you?" I spin around.

"Right here, standing on the toilet. I didn't want those two girls to see me."

"God, Ellie. Would you just get out here and tell me what you want?" My face burns, I'm that pissed off. "Why do you always have to be so dramatic? Why is everything always such …"

When she steps out of the stall, I gasp. Her bottom lip is split and puffy. Blood is trickling onto her chin. Her eyes are red, her cheeks soaked with tears.

"What the hell *happened* to you?" I practically shout.

"Shhh. I don't want anyone to hear us."

"But when did you even get in here?"

"I snuck through the halls during first period. Nobody saw me." She sniffs hard and wipes her face with a wad of toilet paper. "You won't even *believe* what happened to me on my way to school this morning, Clems."

"Try me," I tell her, even though she's probably right. I likely won't believe her. "You have about two minutes. *Go*!"

"Clemen*tine*!" She snuffles loudly. "Why are you being so *mean*!"

Me being mean! "Minute-and-a-half left …"

"Okay, so when I was walking to school this morning, this weird guy I never saw before came out of nowhere and tried to grab my backpack. So, I fought back, and he, like, *punched* me in the mouth and swore at me!"

"Really."

"Then he took off without it. Because I hung on so hard. And I was so *totally* freaked out, that I just walked around for most of first period, crying my *butt* off. And then I came to school."

"Really."

The second-period bell buzzes above our heads. Ellie sniffs again. "And here I am."

"*Uh-huh*. So, Ellie, when you're ready to tell me the truth about what *really* happened to you this morning, just text me, okay?"

I turn around and walk straight out of the washroom without looking back. I have a feeling that for reasons I don't completely understand, I'm starting to get the upper hand with this girl.

Deep down I think I know exactly what happened to Ellie. But I'm not quite ready to let myself go there yet.

THE NEXT TEXT pops up just before lunchtime.

I think I'm ready Clems. Meet me in front of the school.

Maybe she's ready, but I'm not so sure that I am. Mostly because I dread hearing the next story, just wondering if it'll be fact or fiction. Curiosity wins though.

I'll be there, I text back.

I'm under the big tree.

The big tree. A sugar maple so brilliant now that its leaves have morphed to orange and gold, that it almost hurts your eyes to look at it on a sunny day like this one. When I get there Ellie's sitting behind the trunk, out of sight of the school, as if she's trying to hide. I sit down beside her and open my lunch. She eyes my ham sandwich, but I don't offer her a bite. Her split lip still looks sore. I try not to stare while I wait for her to say something.

"So, what do you think really happened to me this morning?" she finally says.

"What I don't *believe* is that you were attacked by a stranger. What I do *hope*, is that you weren't smacked around by someone you know. It has to be one or the other though, right?"

She nods and stares into space for at least a full minute.

"Okay, so I had a huge fight with my mom," she says. "About Mac. And she freaked."

My sandwich feels very dry in my mouth. "Come *on*. She didn't hit you."

She sort of nods again, but won't look me in the eye.

"Yelled at me to get my act together this morning. Slapped me when I mouthed off and shoved her. So I ran out of the house and wandered around instead of coming to school in time for first period. She's being such a bitch. So, anyway, are we on for this weekend or what?"

"That's *it*? That's all you're giving me, and you expect me to be good with it?" There has got to be way more to this than she's willing to share. The Mrs. Denton that I've known for ages would never, ever strike her daughter. I stare at Ellie and wait.

"Yes, that's it. Why does she have to be such a jerk about me having a boyfriend?" Annoying pouty mouth. "She's hated Mac ever since we got together. And she's *always* pissed with me."

"Clearly your mom's sick of the way you've been acting, Ellie. And you just keep on finding new ways to make her crazy. But I don't believe that she hit you."

"My mother doesn't get me, won't even try, doesn't even care. So are you helping me out or what? Can I stay at your place Friday night?" Now her voice is sweet and soft and desperate. She doesn't care if I believe her story. She just wants me to feel bad for her, so I'll say yes.

I don't even have to think twice about my answer. "Nope." I stand up. "Not this time. I don't feel like watching you crash and burn."

Stunned silence for a moment. "You know what, *Clem*?" A hard and furious voice. "You are a complete and total —"

I hold up my hand. "Don't even say it."

Ellie gets up slowly and brushes off the seat of her jeans.

"Okay, then. Guess it's time for me to give up everything I know. About what happened with you and Kit that night." She crosses her arms and aims her stormy brown eyes at mine.

I give her my best Cheshire Cat smile. "Go right ahead. Because deep down I have a feeling you know more about what happened that night than I do. And you're even more afraid than I am for the truth to come out. So just go for it. *Tell* somebody. Give it *all* up, once and for all, Ellie. I *dare* you."

By the change in her face, I know I've nailed it. Her smug air of confidence and control dissolves right before my eyes. For a fleeting moment she looks a bit like the old Ellie I once knew, the girl I actually cared about a lot.

"You are so full of crap." A tremor to her voice now. "You make me absolutely sick." Then something shifts in her face, and she half smiles. "Kit's mom is still looking for answers. Maybe it's time for the truth to finally come out about what Spencer did to Kit that night."

A mild shockwave buzzes through my body. I narrow my eyes. "What's that supposed to mean, Ellie? That you're going to feed Ms. Stitski a bunch of lies? Just like you do to everyone else?"

She looks stunned for a second and stands there blinking before gaining her composure. "Well, I guess it means whatever you want it to mean, Clementine," she says.

Then she walks off toward the school doors, leaving me there knowing that things have definitely changed between the two of us, that they might be even worse now. Because I have a sinking feeling I know exactly who started that fight rumour. But why, Ellie? *Why?*

"YOU ABSOLUTELY SURE you're ready for this, Clem?"

I might never be, but Jake is gazing at me so intently, all I can do is nod. I'm willing to bet he's hoping I'll say no, so he can be off the hook, too. But it's something we need to do.

I still haven't shared what Ellie and I said to each other today. I'm afraid he'd totally lose it if he knew that Spencer's name came up. And besides, maybe she was only calling my bluff, trying to scare me as much as I scared her when I dared her to come clean. She could be faking me out by trying to prove that she has the guts to put the blame on Spencer, and eventually maybe even me, since she knows my secret. If only I could find out what she's really hiding behind all those masks she wears.

"I'm ready. Let's do this before we totally chicken out again," I say.

We climb on the bus together. Then we're on our way toward the sprawling subdivision where Kit once lived, at the edge of town, not too far from the quarry. We're taking our chances that Ms. Stitski will be home from her office, or the courthouse, or wherever it is that she spends her busy days.

The usual landmarks, streets, churches, and plazas give way to unfamiliar surroundings. I've never had any reason to venture into this part of town. Its opulence is totally intimidating. Kit always had to take the school bus to school. I'm close enough to walk or ride my bike.

Twenty minutes later, the bus rumbles away, leaving us standing on a strange corner in a strange place. I feel like yelling, *Wait. Come back!*

THE QUARRY ESTATES, reads the bronze-on-granite sign at the entranceway to the subdivision. We're surrounded by hulking mansions with impressively landscaped gardens and expensive cars parked in front of double garages. Pool slides jut up above the tops of fences.

"God, you could practically fit four of my house into one of these," I say. "That one looks like a spooky castle, doesn't it?" I point at a looming mansion with grey stones and turrets.

Almost ominously, the sun disappears behind a cloud, and I shiver just a little.

"So this is the street. What number are we looking for?" Jake asks.

"Sixteen Breezy Lane."

"Funny thing about the street names here, huh?" Jake says.

I'd been thinking the same thing as we came in on the bus. We'd passed Shady Trail, Clover Court, and Meadow Crescent. They sounded more like something you'd find in a quaint country village than this place.

Quarry Estates almost seems like a gated community, where Jake and I don't belong. It's like at any moment security guards might rush us and tell us we're trespassing. Nearby, a couple of dogs bark from a backyard, as if they're warning us that it might be wise to leave.

"It's that way," Jake says. Then he grabs my hand and starts walking.

9

WE STAND AT the end of the wide flagstone walkway leading to the front entrance. A BMW is parked in the driveway. There are sculpted shrubs and hedges, and a rose garden with a few last vividly red blooms. Great chunks of granite rock are placed at angles around the property. It sure isn't wild and tangled like our front yard at home.

"Looks like Edward Scissorhands is the gardener here," I tell Jake with a nervous laugh.

The house is stone and stucco with a massive wooden front door. It looks like a country manor. On the main floor all the drapes are drawn, like the house has its eyes closed. A lot of the other places around here look the same. Beautiful but lifeless. A sleeping community.

Each of them has a security warning sticker on the window. THIS PROPERTY PROTECTED BY …

Are security cameras taping us from secret locations?

Beside me, Jake sighs. "Let's do this," he says, and we both walk on.

"Get *lost*. We don't *want* any."

A kid's voice, coming from an upstairs window. Kit's little brother. How did he even notice us from up there? Unless he was watching through the window.

"Kevin? Is that you?" I manage to stammer.

A long, heavy pause. "Who are *you*?"

"Old friends of your brother." Jake's voice sounds way more confident than mine. "We went to school with him."

"Well, he's *dead*. So, what the hell do you want?"

The word *dead*, and the way he says it, makes my stomach flip.

What *do* we want, really? Maybe it was a total mistake to come here today. We really don't have a solid plan. Are we just looking for answers to put our own minds at ease? Will Ms. Stitski see right through us, even if we try to explain why we haven't spoken to her sooner, why we skipped out on the memorial and funeral back in June?

"We … we just wanted to try and explain a few things," I say to the face in the window. "Is your mom home? Can we talk to her, just for a few minutes?"

"About what?"

"Um …" I look frantically at Jake, and he shrugs. "About your brother, and how we went to school with him. About how much we liked him."

There's a long pause, like he's considering. "Nope. She's busy. Take a hike."

A finger flips us the bird. Kevin is the Keeper of the Castle, protecting his mother from intruders like us. I can barely begin to imagine how they're both still feeling. Maybe talking about Kit will only make things worse, conjure up their own "horrible shadows."

I can't really blame Kevin for sending us away.

"Guess we should just go home now," I say to Jake.

He nods at me. "We should have known. But at least we tried."

"Yeah, at least that's something."

I, for one, am filled with an overwhelming sense of relief as we turn and head back to the bus stop. I was utterly terrified to face Kevin and his mom. Never in my life have I had to come up with the right words to offer grieving people, and I'm practically ecstatic about this opportunity to put it off for a while longer.

"When's the next bus?" I ask as Jake checks the schedule on his phone.

"Oh, crap, not for about twenty minutes." He sounds as disappointed as I feel.

"Hey! You guys! Wait a second!"

The voice from the window again. Jake and I stop on the sidewalk and look back. A head is sticking out now. The relief hisses out of me like a deflating balloon.

"Come back. My mom says she wants to talk."

She's waiting for us at the front door, and by the way her arms are crossed, there is *no way* we're getting inside. Small mercies. It's the absolute last place on earth I want to go right now. Ms. Stitski is dressed casually in slim jeans and a rust-coloured tunic. She looks older than she probably should, with lines etched into her face that clearly haven't come from smiling. Kevin's head is still sticking through the upstairs window like a castle gargoyle.

"You okay, Ma?" he calls down.

"Go do some homework, Kevin." She stares at us with wary eyes. "What do you two have to say for yourselves this afternoon?"

When you're a kid, they give you shots to prevent lockjaw. That obviously isn't working for me right now. My mouth refuses to open, even as Jake is nudging me to speak.

"*Well?* Do you have something you'd like to share? Speak up or I'm going back inside."

"Please, don't do that Ms. Stitski," I finally manage to get out. "We really want to talk to you. About what happened after that night. And some other stuff."

Her eyes get narrower. "What happened *after* that night? What I want to know is what happened *on* that night, when my son drowned. When everyone abandoned him. There's nothing left to say about what came *after*, is there?" She looks up. Half of Kevin is hanging out the window. "Get inside. *Now!*" And he does. Fast.

"It's just that …" How to even say this? "Well, Jake and I … I'm Clementine, by the way … we didn't go to the vigil at the quarry. Or to Kit's funeral. And we're feeling awful about it."

Mrs. Stitski's jaw tightens, and she tilts her head. "Feeling awful about it? My heart bleeds for you. I didn't go to the vigil at the quarry either. Because it was really just for Kit's so-called friends, wasn't it? And I don't have a clue who was at his funeral. So is that it? Are we done here?"

"No," Jake says. Thank god, because I'm tongue-tied again. "First of all we want to apologize for not being at the funeral. And for not coming to see you sooner."

"Do you really think that matters to me? Or to Kevin? *Nothing* matters now."

Her words sting because they're so true. How can anything matter more than Kit? I almost feel his ghost again. Is it watching through his bedroom window, a vacant room now, which must shriek out sadness? I'm more than half afraid to look, just in case.

Then suddenly I know what to say.

"We know it can't possibly matter more than Kit." When I say his name, she flinches slightly. "Nothing ever can. But we just wanted you to know how much he mattered to us."

Mrs. Stitski looks down at her sandal-clad feet, then back at us.

"Come inside," she says. "I'm just making tea."

At this moment there is *nothing* I would like more than to be a coward and bolt in the other direction, away from the yawning darkness behind that door. But Jake grabs my arm before I can even think twice about making a move.

"We'd love to," he says, and we follow her through the door.

Inside seems to be all polished wood and marble. It even smells rich. There's one of those curved staircases, like you see in movies, and what must be fine art on all of the walls. On every flat surface, there are vases and flowers, sculptures and carvings. I can't imagine having to dust in there, but then I realize that Ms. Stitski probably has a cleaning lady to do those things for her.

Kit's picture jumps out at me from everywhere I look, twisting my gut. He's still here, in every room of this house, asking not to be forgotten.

We sit at an antique kitchen table, probably made of pine. The kind my mom has on her wish list. None of the china teacups match, but each is pretty in its own way. Ms. Stitski pours our tea from a flowered pot, then sits down across from us with her elbows on the table.

"So, what exactly was it that you wanted to say? It's Clementine and Jake, right?" Her green eyes are red-rimmed and squinty, as if she never gets enough sleep.

I take a sip and almost choke when it burns going down. Ms. Stitski pours some more milk into my cup to cool it down. Just like my own mom would do.

"I wanted to go to the funeral." I stare into my tea. "But I couldn't face you or Kevin. I had no clue what to say that would make things better."

I watch Ms. Stitski add a teaspoon of honey to her own teacup, and a lot of milk.

"You were in a play with Kit, back in middle school, weren't you, Clementine?" she says as she stirs, and I look straight at her. When our eyes meet across the table, I try to smile.

"Yes. Kit was hilarious playing Sam-I-Am, wasn't he? Walking across the stage with that sign. And randomly showing up when he wasn't supposed to. The whole audience cracked up. And the way he stole the mic from the drama teacher and started thanking everyone at the end of the show." The memory helps me genuinely smile.

"I used to let him try my skateboard," Jake is grinning himself now. "He wiped out a few times. I was always worried he'd hurt himself. But he never did."

"Oh, so *you're* the guy," she says. "Kit told me about you. He really liked you."

"He did?" Jake looks surprised.

"He knew everyone's name at middle school, I swear." Ms. Stitski spins her teaspoon on the table. "He was always great with names. And times tables. Used to help

Kevin with math. And science, too. So much that it drove the poor kid nuts!"

When she looks up at us her eyes are watery. "Now isn't this so much better than coming here and telling me you're sorry you missed the funeral? I'd rather hear your personal stories about Kit than apologies for something that doesn't even matter anymore. I don't want to forget him, or for everyone else to, either." She sniffles, wipes her eyes. "God, I miss that kid so much. He was a total challenge, frustrating and inspiring. And I truly loved every minute of it."

My throat aches, and I can't hang on to it anymore. I choke out a sob. Ms. Stitski passes me a box of tissues. I pull out a couple of pieces and dab at my eyes and nose.

"Look, I don't want to sit here and burden you with my grief," she says. "We're all dealing with this in our own way. Like Kevin. He's acting out, stays home a lot, and the school keeps calling. But with everything else on my plate right now, I'm letting him have some space, take his own time to heal. That works best for both of us."

A tear slips from my eye, and I brush it away. All my fears, for all those months, have come to this: a sad woman who's working through her terrible grief. And her remaining son, who's doing his best to keep strangers away and protect their fragile feelings.

She actually appreciates that we've shared our memories of Kit.

Then she leans forward on her elbows again. And something odd happens, something starts to change. Her face begins to morph, to harden, as though she's struggling to overcome the vulnerability she just let loose. As if she needs to trap it again, so she can take control of the situation. The room feels charged with a different sort of energy now, and it's no longer sadness.

"So, Clementine, Jake, there's no denying I'm still curious," she says, her eyes wide and intense as she explores our faces. Probing for clues and answers? "You were at the assembly Friday. You must be here for another reason. What is it? Tell me what you know. You were there that night, weren't you."

Gulp. I *do not* want to try and find out if she has any more clues about what happened that night. Because our visit here has turned into something else. Something better than that. Before I can open my mouth, though, Jake touches my hand, and when I look over, he nods.

"We honestly wish we had more to give you," he says.

She sits there quietly appraising us, as though she's trying to get a reading, to gauge our honesty. "But how did he wind up in the water? I need to find out what *really* happened. In order to reach some state of peace. Do you understand that?"

Under the table, Jake nudges me with his knee.

"I do understand that, but we don't know anything Ms. Stitski. Has anyone new come forward? Did you get any new clues after the assembly?" *There.* I got something out, at least.

She sits up straight, and she takes a sip of tea.

"No, that hasn't happened. Not yet. Look, I want this solved." She sets her cup down with a clatter. "Because someone *else* was there and knows something." Her nostrils flare, jaw juts outward. "That *kid* was there, the one who liked to give him a hard time. I've heard something about a fight between them. So, I can't help thinking that maybe he said something, did something that upset Kit. What if he even pushed Kit over the edge, into the water?"

Uh-oh. I look over at Jake, willing him to keep quiet, but I can see it won't work.

"You're right. My friend Spencer *was* there that night," Jake says in his flat voice. "But I can guarantee that he never hurt Kit, and he had nothing to do with your son disappearing."

Instant suspicion in her eyes. When she stands up, I wish I could will myself to vanish.

"Ah, I *get* it now. You're *protecting* him aren't you? Why did you really come here today? To somehow exonerate yourselves, as well as him? Because you two *really do* know more than you're saying? Don't you?"

"No, that's not it at all," I tell her.

"If the two of you don't have anything else to offer, then I think it's time for you to go. Kevin, I know you're hiding out in the hallway, listening. Please take them to the door."

Kevin sticks his head around the corner, and his mother rolls her eyes. Then she turns abruptly and walks off through a doorway into another part of the house. Kevin stares at us. He has a mess of curly hair, just like Kit had. He's practically a mini-version of his brother. His mother must have trouble looking at him sometimes.

"That way, right?" I point, and he nods then leads us around a corner and down the hall. "So, your brother used to help you out at school, huh?" I say when we reach the front door.

"Yeah, I mostly suck at math and science," he says.

"So does my brother, Zach. He's in grade eight, and I have to help him out all the time. I'm kind of geeky."

"Wait. Is your brother Zach Sanford?" Kevin's eyes grow wide. "He goes to my school. He's so cool."

"So *cool*?" I laugh. "That's questionable. So you know him, huh? You want to come to the library and study with him some time, maybe? I can help you, too, you know."

"Really? That would be *sweet*," he says.

"Okay, so how about this coming Sunday? Meet us at the library. I'll get Zach to let you know what time."

"Awesome-sauce!" Then he turns to Jake. "I've seen you skateboarding around town," he says. "I've got one, too. I kind of suck at it. But I think I'm getting better. Maybe a little anyway." He grabs a skateboard out of a closet and shows it to Jake.

"Well, that's cool," Jake says with a legit smile as he examines it and spins a wheel. "I started when I was your age. Had an Element deck once, too. Takes a ton of practice."

"Maybe I'd get some if my mom would let me out of her sight once in a while. She makes me wear a helmet, too." Kevin grimaces as if he's ashamed.

"Yeah, most kids are wearing 'em nowadays," Jake says to make him feel better. "Probably a good plan, right, Clem? Because you never know when you might wipe out."

He winks at me, and I smile.

Kevin opens the front door, but suddenly he turns and points at something. "See that?"

Jake and I look.

"That backpack in the corner?" he says, and we both nod. "That's Kit's. It's been sitting right there for four months. Right where he dropped it last June. Mom won't put it away. It's like she's still hoping he'll come home."

"Wow, that sucks," Jake manages to murmur, then stands there blinking.

"God, I'm so sorry to hear that, Kevin," I say. "It must be hard."

"Yeah." Kevin sighs as we head out the door. "I just wish my mom would quit blaming herself. See you Sunday, Clem."

He shuts the door and locks it. At the end of the walkway, Jake grabs my arm.

"Did you hear what Kevin just said?"

"About her blaming herself? Yeah, I heard," I tell him. "Still trying to process it. But all of a sudden, everything is starting to make a little more sense."

10

FOR THE ENTIRE bus ride home, Jake and I hold hands. Neither of us says a word, we just stare straight ahead, tangled up in our own thoughts.

I can't help wondering what it means, that our fingers are still laced together on the seat between us. Is he fixated on the same thing? Is he holding on because he's still in recovery mode after our encounter with Ms. Stitski? Or because he likes it? Likes me?

Whatever it is, if there's ever been a better time to ask him to the Sadie Hawkins, this is it. And I decide that I will, as soon as we get off the bus.

When the bus rumbles to a stop back in our own neighbourhood, we're still holding hands. It roars off and leaves us standing on the corner in the same intersection where I knocked him flying with my backpack.

Now, I tell myself, but before I can speak, he grabs hold of my other hand. Then he gazes straight into my face: no shifty, blinking eyes.

"Look, Clem, this is probably a lame thing to do after what just happened with Kit's mom. I mean, it's like I'm totally milking a brutal situation. But I was wondering if you … if you haven't asked anyone yet, if maybe you'd …"

"Yes, I will. Definitely a yes."

"But you don't even know what I was —"

"Yes, I'll go to the Sadie Hawkins with you Saturday. Or should I say, will you come with me? I mean, that's how it's supposed to work, right?"

Jake's serious face dissolves into a smile. "Whew, I was thinking about it for the whole bus ride, so scared you'd say no."

"Great minds think alike," I say. "And the thing is, I was sure someone would have asked you already."

"Someone did." He grins. "A couple of girls, actually. I said no because I was waiting for you. And I seriously hoped that you hadn't already asked someone yourself."

When his fingertips brush my cheek, that's it. I'm instantly smitten. Jake was waiting for *me*!

But I need to tell him what happened with Ellie today. I can't put it off any longer. We have to be totally honest with each other now.

"Jake, something else happened today. Something that could raise the stakes." I hold both of his hands in mine. "Just listen, and let me finish, okay?"

He listens, and he doesn't even move as the news about Ellie's threat sinks in. Then he clenches his jaws and his nostrils flare like a furious bull's.

"It was *her*. She's the one who started that fight rumour."

"Yeah, I think so, Jake. But I promise you, somehow we're going to figure out why."

"Sure hope you're right," he says as a hint of calmness settles over his taut features.

We set off slowly for home, making new plans along the way. First, we want to find a measure of closure for ourselves. To say our own apologies and goodbyes to Kit.

Second, we need to try and figure out who else might know more about what happened to Kit at the field party. We need to beat Ms. Stitski at her blame game. Because as much as we feel sorry for her, she seems more than eager to find someone else to point the finger at for her son's awful death. Prime suspect in her eyes being Spencer — thanks to Ellie.

His name needs clearing whether I like him or not. I've actually reached the point of feeling sorry for him — how can someone so young get so messed up? He must have plenty of his own crappy issues to deal with. And maybe if we figure out what really happened to Kit, we can take our information to the police and get Spencer off Ms. Stitski's hit list. That's third. Figure out what Ellie knows, and why she's trying to frame Spencer.

I'm not sure we accomplished what we set out to do on our visit to the Stitskis' place, but one thing is undeniable. We're getting closer to a measure of closure. It already seems as if a heaviness has lifted just by spending some time with Kit's family. Because as much as Kit's mom is still looking for answers, just meeting with her has answered a few questions for Jake and me. She is *not* about to let this thing go. And maybe Kevin provided a missing piece of the puzzle for us, just by admitting that she won't stop blaming herself. Maybe that's why she's so determined to blame someone else for what went wrong that night.

The best thing about the whole experience is that I think I made Kevin happy by offering to help him out with science. At least I got past the Keeper of the Castle, and managed to earn his trust. Oh, and the dance, going with Jake. Best part of the whole *year* so far!

AT DINNER THAT evening, I explain to Mom, Dad, and Zach about what happened when we visited Kit's mom. I tell them about how Jake and I decided we should meet with Kit's family once and for all, because we've never really had a chance to talk to them, and to tell them how well we knew Kit. And how much we appreciated his sweet nature. I also describe the heavy sadness that lingers in their beautiful home, especially with pictures of Kit everywhere we looked. And how I offered to help Kevin with his studies. They listen in dismay to every word.

"That took a lot of nerve, honey," Mom says when I'm done. "And it's very helpful to me, too. At least we know why Ms. Stitski won't answer her phone. Maybe we should send a social worker to the door at some point, in case she'd like to talk."

"I guess, if you need to try something. But Kevin stands guard at that house. So good luck to anyone who tries to get inside." I smile at the memory.

Zach is trying not to scowl. "Will you still help *me* with science and math?" Figures my brother would worry about something like that. I nod to reassure him.

Dad is still staring at me and smiling wide. "I'm proud of you, Clems. That was a very good thing you did today."

It's bittersweet, the thought of it, just remembering that Jake and I had gone there seeking clues, only to leave with a better understanding of how grief is affecting Kit's family. "I'll tell you one thing for sure, Dad. It was the hardest thing I've ever done in my entire life."

WHEN I TURN my phone back on after the family non-line time, there's still nothing from Ellie. I must still make her "absolutely sick."

Knowing Ellie, and how sketchy she's been acting lately, I'm certain she has something nasty up her sleeve as payback. Her threat to expose Spencer might be part of her plan, but that's getting pretty worn out now, since there's no actual proof that he did anything. So, what if she decides to throw *me* under the bus, as some twisted sense of revenge?

That story about her mom smacking her is *still* eating at me. I couldn't ever imagine my mom being furious enough to slap me that way. But then again, my family hasn't been through what the Denton family has. Ellie's mom is dealing with a major personal struggle. And having a daughter like Ellie, well, it has to be a huge challenge. Especially with the way she's been acting lately. That's not a reason to hit her, because there's *never* a good enough reason for doing something so awful. But if it's true, maybe Ellie should tell someone. And if it's not, then who is she protecting? God, she's been so unreliable lately that it's too confusing to even think about.

I hear from Jake, though, which makes for a perfect distraction. His message is waiting as soon as my screen lights up.

Back online yet? he asks.

Yup. You still there?

Yup, So we still doing this thing tomorrow after school?

My stomach flips at the thought. We have to. To start finding some closure, like we said. Don't forget to bring a candle. Doesn't matter if it isn't dark out. It's symbolic.

It's already in my backpack, he tells me. And matches ☺

We text about other stuff for a while after, and we plan our costumes for the Sadie Hawkins, since it's a masquerade. We figure we should go as some sort of superhero team, but haven't figured it out yet. Then I sign off for the night. I still have homework to do, and it's getting late.

It's hard not to stay fixated on Jake, though.

Is it the uneasy bond we share that prompted him to grab my hand today? To invite me to the Sadie Hawkins? If he feels anything stronger for me, I haven't really picked up on it too much yet. But the fact that he turned down other girls because he was waiting for me is a very good sign! At least we have the dance to look forward to.

Because of our decision to try and reach some state of peace ourselves, just like Ms. Stitski and Kevin are doing, we've decided to hold our own, private, candlelit memorial at the quarry tomorrow after school to say a proper goodbye to Kit. How will I be able to focus on anything else until then?

BUT FOCUS I must. I have no choice. First, there's a pop quiz in health, ugh.

Then there's an announcement from Ms. Raven in theatre arts class. She wants us to produce a revue by the middle of next month. She knows we all have our phones on us, and she often lets us use them as a means of instant research. As soon as she says the word "revue," she tells us to search the meaning. We all do it. Then groans all around!

She points at me. "Read it out loud, Clementine."

"A light theatrical entertainment consisting of short sketches, songs, and dances," I read.

Again, loud groans.

Ms. Raven smiles at all of us. We're spread around the stage floor, where we always start class with strange drama exercises, like floating in bubbles, or pretending we're some sort of mythical animals. Even now Ms. Raven tiptoes around, weaving between us, almost as if she's doing ballet. She's truly the picture of grace.

"Some of you excel at singing, others at dance. Others still prefer to act. I want you to pool your talents. Break up into groups, depending on your specialties, and put something together. It only has to be brief. But first you need to decide on a theme. And you have to figure out a democratic way to choose it, too."

I glance toward Ellie, for about the tenth time since drama class started. She still won't look my way, and she's sitting as far away as possible across the stage. She's being very quiet. Her split lip has settled down; it looks like nothing more than a crack now. Aubrey, on the other hand, is squirming madly beside me.

"This is *so* cool. I totally love singing *and* dancing."

I can only sigh. I wish I could feel excited about it, too. But the messed-up part of my life is undermining the good stuff. Like I don't have enough to stress out about already. Now this.

We listen as Ms. Raven explains the rules for choosing a revue theme. By next week, anyone who comes up with an idea has to present it. Then we'll all vote and take it from there.

My cluttered mind can't possibly inspire me with a half-decent idea before then. But what a relief that I can leave the thinking to somebody else. All I have to do is vote on the theme I like best. At least *one* thing is going my way for a change.

It helps make up for being obsessed with visiting the quarry after school. During every class, as each teacher drones on, my mind won't stop straying to that desolate spot where Kit died. And the candle in my backpack, waiting to be lit.

"WHY DO I feel like I'm going to a funeral?" Jake says beside me.

"Yeah, I know what you mean. We are, sort of, aren't we? This'll be tough."

We've just gotten off the bus on the other side of town, the closest stop to the quarry. We still have to walk about ten minutes. The last time I was here, I was riding my bike through the balmy late-night darkness in the opposite direction, away from the quarry. I'd left Ellie behind, already wrapped around Mac, so thrilled that he'd finally noticed her after a couple of years of crushing on him, and I was sure she'd never even notice I was gone.

That night I felt completely abandoned by her and resentful because Jake didn't speak to me the entire time. Basically, I was feeling sorry for myself. As I'd madly pedalled, I contrived my lie for my parents, about feeling sick at Ellie's place and riding my bike home from there. I was starting to build a whole mountain of lies, and already feeling crappy about it. The last person on my mind was Kit.

What a difference four months can make. I haven't stopped thinking of him since.

Jake and I pause at the end of the rutted gravel pathway leading to the party spot. The area is flat and weedy, with stunted trees and bushes. It's surrounded by mounds of broken rock and larger ridges of earth, where small avalanches of dirt and gravel have broken loose.

This quarry has been abandoned for as long as I can remember. Under a cloudy, late-October sky, with nothing but the sound of distant traffic and the forlorn cawing of crows, I can't help but shudder. It's almost worse than being in his house, because that was the place where he lived. And this? Well, this is the place where he died.

"Let's just get it over with," I say, then start to walk in the direction of the last spot I ever saw Kit alive, not far from the quarry's edge.

Jake is right beside me. Everything looks different in the daylight. Empty and desolate without the blaring music and dancing flames, the whoops and shrieks, and the swarm of writhing bodies. Broken bottles and crushed cans still litter the charred remains of the bonfire. I can barely even glance at it without seeing Kit's face in the firelight's flickering shadows.

I remember his distress because he had to go to the washroom. Then the back of him disappearing into a clump of trees. Too close to the place where the quarry dropped off. Then me looking back toward Jake, hoping he might notice me for a change. Forgetting about Kit instead of looking out for him.

I stop and clench my fists.

"I was so *stupid* that night." I sob as a couple of uninvited tears squeeze out.

Jake slides his arm around my shoulder and tries to pull me toward his chest. "You've got to stop blaming yourself, Clems."

I shake myself free and keep on walking. If he only *knew* how stupid I was, how stuck I was on keeping my eyes on him, and totally forgetting about Kit, he wouldn't even want to touch me. We stop at the edge of the quarry. It isn't so steep a drop, but the rock ledge is crumbly, and if you lost your footing in the dark, you could slide down into watery oblivion. If you bashed your head on the way down, and the water swallowed you up …

"Let's go down there," Jake says, and I turn to stare at him.

"Seriously? I'm not even sure I can do that."

"We have to. We should get close to the last place he ever breathed before we light our candles." Jake grabs my hand. "Come on. We'll go down backwards, slowly."

He crouches at the edge, then turns around and starts climbing in a sort of backwards crab walk down the side of the quarry. The hump of his backpack looks like the crab shell. When I tell him that, he looks up at me and smirks. Then he tells me to start climbing. So, I do it.

It's slow going, especially whenever the rock crumbles away under my feet. So rough and jagged, and hard on the hands. Plants sprout from the quarry wall, and I try to grab hold. Sometimes they come away in my hands, and I slip. I can only imagine Kit's reckless tumble into the water below that night, the shock and pain. I try not to think about that, or to look down on the way to the bottom.

"Careful," Jake says from below me. "There's a tricky spot right —"

And then my foot slips, and I slide down on my belly for about a metre. My shirt slides up, and the rock scrapes at my stomach and tries to bite through my jeans. Wincing, I grope frantically for something to grip. I finally grab a random root and hang on tightly.

"Clems! You okay?"

"Ow, ow, ow," I say through my teeth. "I think so."

When I dare to glance over my shoulder, I realize that I'm not even two metres from the bottom, where Jake waits on a narrow ledge beside the deep pool of water. The place where Kit died. Then I look back at my handhold, a clump of twisted roots sticking out from the rock face like a helpful hand. Something else besides my hand is tangled up in it. I snatch it, and lower myself carefully to the spot where Jake is. Then I look at what I'm holding.

A broken wristwatch.

11

I HOLD THE watch out, and Jake takes it carefully in his hand.

"A wristwatch? That's bizarre."

"Yeah, and it looks a lot like one Ellie wears. She likes it because of the glittering gemstones and coloured beads on the strap. Says it goes with everything she owns. Too bad about the cracked crystal on the face."

"So, what's it doing way down here?"

"No clue." When he hands it back, I tuck it into my pocket. "Maybe I can get it fixed or something." I lift my shirt and peek at my belly. The raw scrape oozes tiny droplets of blood. When Jake sees, he grimaces.

"Ouch," he says, and I shrug.

There's a sound like the scrabbling of shoes on rock, then a shower of crumbled stone bounces off the rock face like a mini-landslide. I look straight up in time to see the back of someone turning away, stepping quickly out of sight. Someone who arrived at the top as we were climbing down? Someone who was watching and listening?

"Hey! Did you see that? Someone was just up there."

"Didn't see anyone, Clem. Just the landslide." I'm left wondering if I imagined the whole thing, but then we both hear an engine rev in the distance, and tires spinning on gravel.

"Who *was* that?" I ask. "Did somebody follow us here?"

"Nobody even knew we were coming here. Weird. Maybe someone else was feeling as lame as us, and came back to have a look?"

"*May*be. But why would they try so hard to avoid being seen? This place is totally creeping me out. Let's just do this and get out of here fast."

Standing beside the tranquil pool of dark water, we light our candles. Then suddenly the sun peeks out from a tear in the clouds, and a robin begins to warble, and it's almost possible to imagine Kit's spirit there watching us.

As I gaze out at the water, I wonder if he can see us. I hope so. Maybe he's looking for closure himself. Spirits in horror movies always seem to haunt the places of their tragic deaths, but I can't imagine Kit being vengeful.

What time is it, Clementine? Kit's voice, or only wind in the branches? I remind myself that this is real life, as goose bumps prickle on the back of my neck.

"Should we say something?" Jake whispers like we're in church.

"Yes. We definitely should. But why don't we just talk about him? Like, remember the Circle of Friends group we formed for him in middle school? And how once a month we'd take him to the movies or bowling?"

"Yeah, I went on a few of those adventures," Jake says. "He used to get so caught up in the movies that he'd talk out loud to the people on the screen and tell them what they should do."

"And get mad if they didn't take his advice! And remember how much Kit liked singing? Especially that

Great Big Sea song, 'Ordinary Day.' Sometimes he used to walk through the hallways singing it."

"Yeah, and he loved dancing, too." Jake smiles. "Remember how at dances he tried to cut in on every couple. Or else just danced alone, boogied like mad. He didn't care if we laughed, because he was laughing, too. He always seemed to be in a good mood."

"Except when he was in a *bad* one," I remind him. "If things didn't go his way, he'd get all stubborn and just sit in the middle of the floor with his arms crossed."

"He'd just park himself wherever," Jake adds. "Middle of the classroom, middle of the cafeteria, or the hall, it didn't matter, and nobody could ever move him!"

"Unless somebody offered him a watch. That was the easiest way to get him to co-operate, remember?" I stand there blinking for a minute, staring at my candle flame flickering in the soft breeze. "Everybody knew that. I'm sure at one point or another, he tried on every watch that anyone ever wore."

"He wore mine a few times," Jake tells me.

"Mine, too. But he always begged to wear Ellie's …" I pull the wristwatch out of my pocket and really look at it. "Because of the beads and stones. He had a rock and mineral collection, remember? So he was crazy about *this* watch."

"Oh, crap." Jake locks his eyes on mine. "You don't think …"

"Yeah. I actually do, Jake. I think that somehow or other Kit got hold of Ellie's watch that night. And somehow or other, Kit and the watch ended up down here."

"But why didn't the cops find the watch back then?"

"It was tangled in those roots. I only saw it because I was looking straight at it. Maybe once they found Kit that day, nothing else mattered. Death by misadventure, remember? It was so obvious that he lost his footing up there and wound up in the water. And this," I stare at Ellie's watch, "has got to be why she started that rumour about Spencer."

AT DINNER THURSDAY evening, I keep my mouth shut about everything.

The rest of them talk about what's going on at Zach's school, like a trip fundraiser selling chocolate bars. Then my mom, who teaches at the same school, explains what happened after the latest meeting about Kevin. Apparently a social worker is going to call on Ms. Stitski early next week. Next, Dad, a history teacher at an arts-oriented high school, gives us a lesson on ancient Greece. Ho-hum.

Throughout it all I stay quiet, missing half the conversation. And getting weird looks.

There's plenty I could talk about, especially with the stinging scrape on my belly as a reminder. But I can't bring myself to discuss our candle memorial or the figure at the top of the ledge. Who *was* that anyway?

I also can't stop thinking about the watch that's still in my pocket. I know that the next thing I have to do is confront Ellie.

Mostly, I stare into my plate of tuna casserole and don't make eye contact. When Zach mumbles something about me being lost in outer space with my alien friends, the look I level at him says more than any words could. He turns away quickly, like he's afraid he might be vaporized. After that they all act as if I'm not even sitting at the table.

Later that evening, during non-line time, I head into the kitchen for a snack. My mom is still in there, leaning on the counter with her back turned, so she doesn't even hear me coming. And I know exactly what she's doing just by the angle of her neck and elbows.

"Hey, Mom, whatcha doin'?" I ask in a perky sing-song voice.

She spins around. "Clem! You startled me. You shouldn't sneak up on people that way." Her phone has already vanished into the pocket of her cardigan.

I offer her a wry smile. "Why? In case 'people' get caught cheating?"

She gives me a sheepish smile back.

"You're right," she admits. "Ten lashes with a wet noodle. I was googling something. But it could have waited. You're saying you haven't cheated yet, Clems, even when you're alone in your bedroom?"

"Yup. Just following house rules. For shame, Mom." I shake my head as though I'm utterly disgusted with her behaviour. "And they say today's *kids* are techno-obsessed!"

"My bad," Mom says, hanging her head.

"God, Mom, you did not *really* just say that."

When she nods, and pulls a gangsta pose, we both crack up.

That night Jake and I text goofy costume ideas until we finally sign off. But my brain is still spinning madly in every direction.

I can't stop thinking about the dance. It's only two days away, and all our costume ideas so far are dumb. And what about that English essay that's due next week — when will I get that done? I have to meet with Kevin at the library on Sunday afternoon to help him with science. Though, who knows if his mom will actually let me help him, after she kicked us out of her house?

After that, my thoughts land momentarily on our theatre arts assignment, and hang out there for a bit. I can't stop thinking about Kit, and everything Jake and I remembered about him at the quarry today. Does everyone else have their own memories tucked away like we do?

And right then and there I hit on an idea. What better way of honouring Kit than by putting together a series of sketches about him? A sort of "Kit Revue." Most kids in our grade knew him in one way or another. Everyone had a soft spot for him, I'm certain of that. He was a loud and lively presence in middle and high school — if he was anywhere nearby, you always knew it.

Before I fall asleep, I write the Kit revue in my head. And even though I didn't want to at first, now I have every intention of presenting my idea for a theme in Ms. Raven's class when the time comes. *Scenes From a Life* — something like that. I even get up to scribble some notes, hoping I'll be able to decipher them tomorrow. And finally, after I have something down on paper, I manage to get to sleep and stay there 'til morning, without a single dream of drowning making my eyes fly open.

FRIDAY MORNING, I'M running late and don't even have time to throw a lunch together before heading to school. My folks are long gone, so I can't beg a ride from them. It used to be so easy when I got driven every day, back when I went to Mom's school, like Zach still does.

I hate getting caught in the hallways after first bell and being sent to pick up a late slip from the office. Some kids are great at avoiding it, but it always seems to backfire on me.

So I leave the house at a run, scuffling along through the crisp leaves littering the sidewalks. After a few blocks I'm out of steam, and I slow to a loping trot as I wind my way through empty streets toward the high school. It's chilly out, hoodie weather, with puffy muffin-top clouds and a goose-bump breeze. With Halloween drawing near, homes are already decorated for trick-or-treaters — jack-o'-lanterns, fluttering ghosts, giant spider webs, and eerie porch scarecrows that look ready to leap to life. It makes me want to hurry.

Only a couple of blocks from the school, a car pulls up beside me. Not just any old car. Mac's blue Wildcat. Ellie's in there, too. I look away and pick up my pace even as the car slows to a crawl beside me. The tinted window slides down.

"Need a lift?" Mac calls through Ellie's window.

"I'm almost there," I tell him without turning my head. Right now those spooky stuffed porch people are starting to look like my best friends.

"Come on. Get in, Clem. We want to talk to you about something."

"Don't have time. The bell's ringing in like five minutes." Faster still, even though my leg muscles are screaming for mercy. I do *not* want to have this conversation. To be walloped by their insane demands about this weekend. I will *not* co-operate anymore.

The car speeds up and screeches around the next corner, out of sight. Thank god. Until I turn that corner, and realize the Wildcat is parked by the curb now, facing the wrong direction. And Mac is leaning against the driver's door with his arms crossed. Waiting for me.

I refuse to meet his eyes, stride right on past, don't even glance toward the car. I'm in the clear, yet my heart is still hammering harder than it should be, because this guy just creeps me out. Then a hand grabs my sleeve and wrenches me around.

Mac's face is too close to mine. It isn't a friendly face. What can Ellie possibly see in his dark probing eyes and tight, angry lips? What is the attraction? And why is he hanging on to my sleeve?

"Come on, just get in the car. We need to ask you something, *okay*?" He's still gripping my sleeve. My gaze flicks over to the passenger seat where Ellie leans forward, watching me with panicky eyes. *Why?*

"Nope, not happening, dude," I say, and hoof him in the shin. When he yelps and lets go of me, I take off running.

The rest of the way to school is a total blur. I keep glancing over my shoulder to check if they're following me. I have absolutely no regrets about kicking him, either. He *so* deserved it. No wonder Ellie is a basketcase these days, latched on to such a jerk.

Now I have an even better idea how she got her bruises and split lip. How can she throw the blame at her mom just to protect this jackass of a guy? How can she live with herself for telling such a humongous lie? Yet she seems to be terrified about something. So why can't she just ditch him? That's what I need to know, now more than ever before.

Just as I reach the school, Mac's car peels away, and I spot Ellie bolting through the front doors as the first bell rings. She's clearly trying to avoid me, and for good reason. But she isn't getting away with this latest incident if I can help it. It's time for her to come clean with me, once and for all, about everything she's hiding.

I try to catch up, but lose sight of her in the hallways when she disappears into the swarm of kids hurrying to homeroom. I already have a plan, though. I slip out an exit, cut across the quad, and step back through another door on the other side of the school. Where I practically slam right into her. Her eyes fly open as she pushes past me.

"Wait!" I catch hold of her arm. "Tell me the truth for once. I want to know what the hell's *really* going on, Ellie!"

"*Nothing.*" She practically shoves me with her shoulder. "I'm gonna be late, and I'm already in trouble for being late twice this week." Her angry eyes bore into mine. "Why are you acting like such a loser all the time?"

She turns away with a scowl and disappears around a corner.

I can't stop wondering who the real loser is. Me, or the girl with the abusive boyfriend?

12

NOT SO EASY to concentrate when you start the day like that. I try my best to focus on my teachers' droning voices, but it's nearly impossible.

In first period, Ellie won't glance my way. All through class she stares into space looking utterly grim, despite a couple of warnings from the teacher. At one point she has her head down on her desk, which makes me wonder if she might be sick.

At lunchtime I don't see her, so I spend my time talking to Aubrey and a couple of other kids about their ideas for the theatre arts revue. I keep quiet about mine, though. I don't want to mention anything until I've got a better idea of the concept. Some of theirs are okay, like a theme based on fairy tales, where we'd perform songs, dances, and scenes from well-known animated shows. I like the Looney Tunes revue, too, based on old cartoons. That could be fun. I'm still stuck on my idea though.

And as I chew my way through my lunch, barely tasting it, I keep one eye on the doorway, watching out for Ellie, but she never shows up. Uneasiness bubbles in my belly. I wait at her locker for a while, but she doesn't show up there either. I ask around, but nobody has seen her since first period.

I run into Jake in the hallway shortly before the bell. He hooks his arm through mine as I'm zooming past. I know there's distress carved into my face because I can actually feel it. Jake sees it, too, I can tell right away. I try to adjust my features to look something like nonchalant. It doesn't work though.

"What's going on?" he says "You look freaked out about something."

"It's Ellie, as usual. I haven't seen her since first period. She didn't show up at lunch. I'm thinking of calling her phone, even though I'd hate for her to think I'm worried."

And I'm just about to call when my text message alert goes off. I hold up one finger and dig into my backpack. I can feel him watching me, and can hardly wait to tell him how I got myself out of my fix with Mac this morning. But as I read the text message on my screen, my stomach does a swan dive to my toes.

Clem, it's Ellie's mom. Do you know where she is?

Oh god, what can I say to Mrs. Denton? I want to at least give her something.

She was at school this morning in first period with me, I text back.

School called. She wasn't in second. Skipping a lot. On probation as it is. Very worried abt her.

I feel I should offer her something, maybe even come up with an excuse. But what's the point? I can't keep lying for my ex-friend and covering her butt as she digs herself into an even deeper hole. Sorry, Mrs. D. Haven't seen or heard from her since.

Thnx. That's all she says. I feel sick right to my core.

"Where the hell did she go?" I ask, staring at Jake. "Why would she leave the school when she's already in a crapload of trouble?"

"Maybe she didn't leave," Jake says. "Maybe she's still around here somewhere."

"Hmmm. Maybe you're right. Sorry, gotta run!"

I head straight for the girls' washroom, just in case. I push through the door. Three girls are just washing up, splashing each other and laughing before drying their hands. One stall door is shut with no feet showing underneath. I sidle into the stall beside it and lock the door. And as soon as the girls leave, I stand on the toilet and peer over.

Sure enough, Ellie's crouched in a huddle on the seat again. She has no clue that I'm looking down at her.

"You moving in here permanently, Ellie?" I try to say it in a nice way because suddenly I just might feel a whole bunch of sorry for her.

She looks up, startled. Her mouth quivers, then she bursts into tears.

"I can't *take* this anymore," she says, gulping through sobs. "I'm so sorry for what Mac did to you this morning."

"I'm *not* sorry for what I did to him. He's a *jackass*. And it wasn't your mom who hurt you, was it? Why did you lie to me?"

Ellie sniffs and shakes her head. "God, you don't really think it was Mac, do you? Because it *wasn't* him. I just hurt myself doing something stupid, that's all. And I didn't want to talk about it. So I just said it was my mom."

"Come on, Ellie. You expect me to believe that? Especially after the rough way he grabbed me beside the car? What the hell was that about? And I saw the bruise on your arm, you know."

Ellie sighs. "There's a perfectly good explanation for that one, too. But you'd never believe it either. Look, Mac's not so bad, really. Once you understand him. His life's totally messed up right now. There's tons of stuff bugging him. And he just kind of has a temper."

"*Huh.* More like a lit fuse. Your mom texted me. She's looking for you. The school called her, you know. She says you're in trouble already. Why'd you skip again today?"

"I couldn't handle going to class. I was scared I'd start crying. And I couldn't go home, in case he's out there somewhere, waiting for me. We had another big fight, and I don't feel like talking to him right now." Huge wet sniffle.

I dig into my pocket and pull out her watch, which I brought to school just in case this opportunity popped up. "Because of this, maybe?" I dangle it in the air over her head.

She gasps. "Where did you find that?" She tries to grab it.

"You were at the quarry yesterday, weren't you? Looking for your watch with Mac. Did you lose this the night Kit died?" I hold it just out of reach. "Is that why you started the rumour about a fight between Kit and Spencer? Was that part of your backup plan? In case you somehow lost control of the situation, and of *me*? And needed someone else to get the blame?"

Bingo. Her face changes quickly; that mist of sadness and angst evaporates. She hops onto the floor and starts spinning tissue off the roll. She uses the wad to wipe her nose and face. Raccoon eyes again. I don't like those eyes.

"What happened to Kit?" I ask.

"You have to give that back to me," she says, ignoring my question. "Honestly, it'll help solve a huge pile of problems for me."

She drops the crumpled wad in the water, flushes it, then steps out of the stall.

"And why's that?" I step out of mine.

"I can't really explain everything right now." Next thing I know she's on her phone, texting madly, a twisted smile on her face. She looks up at me again and holds out her hand.

I shove the watch into my pocket.

"Come on, Clem. I *need* to have it back, like right now."

"So, how did it wind up where I found it, *Els*? Hah... wind up! Get it?" After all the crap she's been putting me through lately, taunting her feels good.

Her mouth tightens, and her eyes well with tears again. She starts blinking fast. "I don't care *where* you found it. I just want it back." She takes a step toward me.

I don't move. "So tell me something. How come Kit and your watch ended up in the same place? Strange coincidence, no?"

I stare at her, daring her to give me an answer. When she doesn't, I turn and walk right out of the washroom door to my next class, just as the bell echoes through the halls.

I know I have her. But I feel more sick about it than triumphant, which makes it hard to focus on my last two classes of the week. Did Ellie go back to class, or is she still hiding out in the washroom? Or did she have the guts to leave the school after all?

And what about Mac? Maybe he isn't who Ellie first thought he was. She's clearly afraid of him, for good reason, but not enough to dump him. What hold does he have on her? What is with Ellie's bizarre behaviour? And why the *hell* did Mac try to yank me into the car with them? This morning I was almost certain it was because he wanted to talk me into covering for Ellie this weekend. But now I'm almost positive it must have been about the watch, and his fear that I found it yesterday.

I can't forget the dark figure at the top of the quarry. And the sound of tires spinning on gravel as a car went speeding away. The Wildcat. It's all starting to become achingly clear. Mac was up there looking for the watch, but took off when he spotted us. Ellie must have been up there with him, too. But what made them go back for the watch now? Did they try to find it earlier and give up? And did Ms. Stitski's speech convince them to try again?

There's something about that watch. Something incriminating? Judging by Ellie's reaction when she saw it in my hand, finding it would mean a whole lot of relief for the two of them. Relief mixed with a desperate rage to get it back.

Ellie's watch has got to be linked to Kit's death. The coincidence is way too obvious. But that still doesn't explain what Kit was doing with it that night, or prove that he even had it at all.

And so, as the rest of my class conjugates verbs aloud with our French teacher, I decide Ellie won't be getting her watch back until I find out the truth.

After school Jake is waiting for me at my locker. In spite of all my misery, my heart does a little dance in my chest at the sight of him standing there looking seriously concerned.

"Did you find her? I texted you, but you never got back to me."

"Oh, I found her all right," I say as I pitch books into my backpack. "Let's get out of here, and I'll fill you in on the latest."

As we wander slowly home, I tell him what happened with Mac that morning. Then I tell him about finding Ellie in the washroom, and my watch theory. Next I tell him everything else. Like how Ellie is trying to force me to cover for her this weekend. That she has bruises on her arm and face, which she blamed on her mom. That I'm positive I know her reason for starting that rumour. I empty out every stupid thing that's been making me crazy, yammering non-stop, as he listens, concerned.

"You know, I've never heard you talk so much," he says when I finally take a breath.

"Yeah, sorry. I had a ton to unload, and nobody else to dump it on. It just feels so good to finally share it with someone. And her story about the bruises, and her split lip? It has to be Mac, but why would she let him treat her that way?"

We're standing on the same corner as earlier this week, where I knocked him off his skateboard. Was that only this week? It feels like ages ago. I still have no idea where I stand with Jake, or where this new relationship is headed. Funny thing, though, I'm less obsessed about it now, more willing to let nature take its course. I almost feel ashamed of all the energy I wasted daydreaming about him for so long, instead of just talking to him. I'm definitely ashamed of how fixated on him I was at the quarry that horrible night. Because if I hadn't been, then the brutal ending to this story might have turned out differently.

Live and learn, as my dad always says when we mess up, only to be met with eye rolls. Maybe he's right after all.

"Glad I could help by being your garbage heap," Jake says. "I feel honoured. I think."

That's when he does it. Leans right over and kisses me. A soft, tentative one, right on the lips. And floating there, in a state of mild shock, I take a chance and kiss him back. He tastes delicious, like spearmint. For a moment I think I might know what flying feels like, and I don't want the kiss to stop. But when it does, we stare at each other and smile.

"I think I like where this is going, Clems," he says. "Hope you do, too."

"You can't even imagine how much," I tell him.

He hugs me with those lanky arms, and I lean in and hug him back, my head tucked into his shoulder. That's when I spot the blue Wildcat as it lurches to a stop at the corner. Before it can speed off, though, the passenger door flies open.

Ellie leaps out, then bolts across the intersection, heading straight for us, as car horns blast from every direction.

13

SHE REACHES US just as the Wildcat pulls a U-turn and roars up to the curb. The tinted window slides down.

"Come on, get your butt back in the car, Ellie," Mac yells out the window. "Why are you acting like such a freakin' maniac right now?"

"Speak for yourself," she yells back.

Then she leans up against Jake and me, cowering like a scared puppy. We stare at Mac and he stares right back.

"If you two are smart you'll stay out of it. You have no clue what you're getting into with that messed-up chick. Or me," he warns us before he speeds off.

When she finally looks at us, Ellie's face is soaked with tears, her eyes bloodshot.

"Okay, so you want to hear what really happened that night?" she asks.

"It's about time," I tell her without a trace of sympathy in my voice.

We grab some snacks at the convenience store, then sit on a bench in front of the plaza. As Ellie finally starts talking, she almost seems to be in a trance, her eyes fixed in the distance as if they're looking into the past.

"So, I ran into Mac that night, like you already know. And we just couldn't let go of each other. It was amazing. We danced and partied with everybody, and after a while he led me away from the bonfire, over to a dark place in the bushes, where we could … well, you know."

She pauses to nibble on a potato chip. I don't want her to stop talking.

"Yeah, we get it, Ellie," I say. "Keep going."

She takes a deep breath. "Okay, so then Kit comes stumbling along after a bit and practically crashes right into us. He starts laughing and saying 'I know what you're doing. I know what you're doing.' And he keeps poking me in the back."

"Yep, that sounds like Kit," Jake says. I touch his arm so he won't say any more.

"So then he spots my watch. The moon was so bright that night, it was even sparkling. And you remember how much he liked the stones, so he starts begging me to try it on. And you know how it is when he grabs hold of your wrist, and won't let go? Well, he started doing that to me, too." She takes a couple of deep, gasping breaths. "And Mac tells me to just give the watch to him, so he'll get lost and leave us alone."

Uh-oh. I'm starting to see where this is going already. I close my eyes and wait for the rest. As if he's sensing my distress, Jake slips his arm around my shoulder.

"So, I give him the stupid watch, just to get rid of him, and he goes running away with it." Her tears fall faster now, but she doesn't wipe them off her cheeks. "And after that Mac and I never even saw him again. And we didn't try to find him either."

"Oh, crap, Ellie," I say.

"So, it's totally *my* fault he died. Not *your* fault, Clems. Mine! And Kit's mom is looking for answers. I've got a few, and if she finds out, she'll think Mac and I are murderers. She'll have us charged, and we'll have to go to jail! She's a freaking lawyer!"

"Giving him your watch doesn't make you a murderer," I tell her in a firm voice, so she'll listen to me. "That doesn't change anything else that happened that night."

Ellie sniffles loud and long. "It totally does, Clem. For me *and* Mac. And you were right. That rumour totally was my backup plan. It was insurance, to stop all this from coming back on us."

"So, you actually believed it was a good idea to screw Spencer over to save your own hides?" Jake shakes his head. He's disgusted by Ellie. "That's just plain sick."

"Sick and pathetic," I say. "You'd say anything to cover your own ass, wouldn't you?"

Ellie slumps forward on the bench and starts sobbing. I look at Jake and shrug because there isn't anything left to say. Nothing can change the awfulness of what happened that night, even if the police did find out what happened with Ellie, Mac, and Kit. We're each at fault in one way or another, the four of us. Ellie and Mac just fill in the last pieces of the puzzle.

I dig the watch out of my pocket as Ellie sits up and wipes off her face. Lately, all she ever seems to do is cry. I hold the watch out.

"You want this back? Maybe you can get it fixed or something."

"God, no." She pushes my hand away. "I never want to look at that thing again. Or Mac! I'm just so sick and tired of everything that's been happening. He actually thinks we should get rid of the stupid watch for good."

"Because it's evidence, and he's scared?" I ask, and she nods. "And you told him I found it. You were texting him in the washroom today, right?"

Another big, fat tear rolls out. "So then he waited for me after school, near my street, and asked me to give him the watch. I said I didn't have it, and he said I needed to get it from you. And he squeezed my wrist and it hurt. And I started getting really scared."

"Oh, cripes." I shake my head. Why did she have to let it get this far? She should have ditched him ages ago. But maybe he didn't let her, because of the secret between them.

"We drove along your route home from school to try to find you. To get the watch back. He was so upset, pounding on the steering wheel and stuff. Acting all sketchy, and it started to scare me even more. When I saw you guys, I pretty much jumped out of his car."

"Sounds like he's getting desperate," Jake says. "He knows that watch can link the two of you to what happened to Kit. And now that we have it, he's probably afraid we'll go to the cops and rat him out."

Ellie just sits there nodding and scrubbing at her smudgy eyes. At that point I decide not to put it off any longer. I need to know for certain right now.

"Okay, so what's the real story about your split lip?" I ask with a challenge in my voice. "Did Mac do that to you? Is he slapping you around Ellie? Because if he is …"

"I already told you. He *didn't* smack me. Mac picked me up on the way to school that morning, and we were goofing around, play-wrestling in the car. My mouth bashed into his forehead. It started bleeding, so I had to wait 'til it stopped, and I was late for class. *That's* why I was crying. I was afraid of getting in trouble again. I didn't tell you the truth because I knew you wouldn't believe it was an accident."

"And the arm thing? That wasn't because of your mom or Mac?" I ask, still skeptical. "I'm finding it hard to believe anything you've told me lately."

"Just a bruise from climbing around at the quarry. We went looking for the watch a few days ago, and I wiped out on the rocks. That's the total truth."

"Yeah, Clem got hurt over there, too." Jake looks at me and winces.

Ellie wipes her nose on her sleeve. "*My* life has been a complete mess ever since June. Because of that watch. You should just give the stupid thing to him and let him do what he needs to with it. And forget about all this, Clems."

Her life has been a mess? "It's way too late for that Ellie. And *I'm* holding on to this watch myself for now."

JAKE AND ELLIE come home with me after that. It's been absolute ages since she's been at my place. She hasn't dropped by all summer long — she was too busy with her so-called boyfriend. It's almost like a homecoming when she steps inside. She looks around at everything familiar, and smiles wide. "I miss your place," she murmurs.

Zach's jaw drops when we all walk in, and for once in his life, he's speechless. Mom's thrilled though. She hugs Ellie twice, then gives me two thumbs-up about Jake behind his back.

Dad's just happy to have new guinea pigs — Friday is the night he likes to try out recipes he's discovered watching food shows and surfing the net.

Tonight he's trying Thai food. He puts us to work making the peanut sauce, cooking glass noodles, and chopping cilantro, carrots, and green onions for the fresh spring rolls. Then we bundle everything in the flimsy rice-paper wraps, which keep on ripping in our untrained hands. Meanwhile, Dad, Mom, and Zach are working on the coconut-chicken curry soup that they're making from scratch. The kitchen smells scrumptious, and our phones stay switched off the whole time. Our guests' phones, too, which they actually agreed to without making a fuss.

It took Ellie a bit of convincing until I explained the upside.

"Huh," she said. "I never thought about it, but I guess it could be freeing, not having to be on call for your friends all the time." She raised one eyebrow.

"Yeah, exactly, Els," I told her. *Or boyfriends you should really just dump.*

And then, joy of joys, we finally get to sit down and eat our amazing Thai dinner!

"Okay, that's it," Jake says between mouthfuls of cold spring roll. "I'm starting this tradition in our family, too." Then he frowns. "Except nobody likes to cook."

"Then I guess you'll have to be the chef," Dad says with a wink. "It's simple, Jake. And if you hang around here often enough, you just might learn something."

An instant blush creeps up my neck. *Really, Dad?*

Ellie won't quit glancing over at her phone, which is

understandable, since it came as a shock to the system the first time I tried it.

"Don't worry, you get used to it after a while," Mom says, patting her hand.

"Or you could cheat," I add. When Mom shoots me a look across the table, I change the subject quick. "Okay, so costumes for tomorrow night, Dad. How about if Jake and I dress as Macbeth and Lady Macbeth? Do you have any costumes in your drama department that you could pinch for us? Your school performs a lot of Shakespeare, doesn't it?"

"We did *Macbeth* last year for the spring show," Dad says. "Maybe if you bribe me by cleaning up this kitchen, I can slip over there tomorrow morning and check out the costume cupboard, borrow something that could work."

"That would be *so* cool," I say, even though Jake's eyebrows just shot up.

"*Seriously?*" He shrugs. "I *guess* that's okay. As long as I don't have to wear a dress."

"Maybe I'll just skip the dance." Ellie gazes into her soup bowl, fiddles with her spoon." I don't even have a date, and it's a Sadie Hawkins, right."

"Yeah, maybe you should just stay home for a change," I agree, feeling very little sympathy for her.

"I don't have a costume anyway." She's staring at me now with pleading eyes.

"Yeah, it's kind of late for that now, Ellie," I remind her.

"But you could go as Banquo's ghost, Ellie," Dad suggests with a huge grin on his face, and I look over and shoot daggers with my eyes. He doesn't even catch on. And of course Ellie's eyes light up.

"*Great* idea, honey," Mom says, smiling at Dad.

"Wow! That would be so cool," Ellie says, a smile starting to form on her face.

"I can check the costume room," Dad says. "I know there's a sort of white cloak with a 'blood-stained' hood covering the entire head. And eyeholes. Like a beefed-up traditional bedsheet ghost costume. Hope nobody's borrowed it already."

"Perfect. And it sure beats hanging out at home with my mom, anyway." She sort of frowns. "Mom's not too thrilled to chill with me these days, either. Guess I kinda can't blame her."

There's no stopping this runaway train now. Looks like Ellie's coming to the dance solo. And right now she *almost* looks like a sad little girl in desperate need of cheering up. And it *almost* seems like she's starting to regret some of the utterly dumb choices she's made lately. Or maybe she's just faking it. It's so hard to tell with her these days.

I still can't imagine what she was thinking. Couldn't she see how badly she'd been messing up? How out of control things were getting? I truly hope this will be a turning point for my old friend, and that she'll actually try to turn things around.

"Okay, Dad," I say. "You have a deal. We'll do the kitchen for you and you get us the costumes."

Dad looks around at the food-prep disaster area that the kitchen has become and smiles. "It's *so* worth it."

While we eat, Mom tells me how Kevin seemed so happy today and how he went up to her and told her about his study plans with me at the library Sunday afternoon.

"He sounded excited about it. And the other teachers agree that it's a great plan. Especially taking your brother along." Mom kisses the top of my head. When I catch Ellie watching us, she looks away.

"Wait, *what*?" Zach says through a mouthful of noodles. "What are you talking about?"

"Well, Zach, I thought it would be nice if you came along too. Kind of like a role model for Kevin. And I told him you'd let him know what time. I really need you there. I promised him."

"*What*? No way. Anyway I'm busy this Sunday."

"You'll think about it? Well that's *great* to hear, Zach." Dad winks at my brother.

Zach nearly chokes, then glares at me across the table.

THAT NIGHT ELLIE and I have our first sleepover in ages. It feels as if we're ten years old again. We even have a pillow fight, jumping back and forth between the twin beds in my room like we used to do back when we were sweet and innocent little kids. Then we give each other manicures and pedicures and start talking our faces off.

"You don't even know how much better I feel now, just coming clean about what happened that night," she says as she brushes Petunia Pizzazz on my toenails.

"Honestly, Els," I wiggle my toes because it tickles, "it's a huge relief for me, too. Just knowing I'm not the only one who's been feeling guilty. I still have freaky nightmares. I just wish you hadn't brought Spencer into the mix."

"I know. Me, too. But I didn't know what else to do, Clem. I was going crazy worrying. You know, sometimes I wonder if Mac and I really like each other, or if we're just stuck together because all this nasty crap happened. Okay, don't wiggle or I'll mess up." She pinches my baby toe, and I yelp. "The whole Kit thing made us totally paranoid. And since Ms. Stitski showed up at the assembly last Friday, things have gotten worse than ever. I wish Mac and I could start over from a different place, a different time. Before all hell broke loose in June."

"Hmmm, maybe you two should take a break for a while, just 'til all this blows over," I tell her, then blow on my toenails to dry them. "It's like you guys are the worst thing to happen to each other. Bet your mom thinks that anyway."

"Yeah, I know what you mean. I promise you, I'm gonna try harder with my mom. I've really been a total bitch with her lately. And I also plan on keeping my distance from Mac until this all blows over. It really is the best thing for both of us. He's getting way too stressed out over everything and he's stressing me out too. But I'm not sure all this will ever completely go away, either. Especially with Kit's mom looking for a scapegoat. And with that watch reminding us. We should just get rid of it like he says, don't you think?"

It's the most earnest I've seen her face in ages. I'm almost proud of her for taking a shot at owning her problems. "I'm not sure yet. It's still evidence. If they ever reopen the investigation, it might be good to have around. Don't worry. It's somewhere safe."

Buried deep in the back of my undies drawer for now.

"Sure hope you're right," Ellie murmurs. "And thanks for not despising me. Or giving up on me." Then she leans over to hug me, and I hug her back for the first time in ages.

After that we watch our fave movie, *The Notebook*, on my laptop.

When we finally turn the lights out, I see her texting in the other bed as my eyes flutter shut. My phone is in the kitchen with Mom's, Dad's, and Zach's, our night-time family pact still intact.

I wake up once when I hear a thump and an "ouch." Ellie's standing in the middle of my room, holding her phone. "What's wrong?" I squint in the glow from her flashlight app.

"Wow, Clems, I was trying to find my way to the washroom in the dark, and I walked straight into your closet and stubbed my toe on something," she says.

"Hah! What a loser!" I laugh, roll over, and snuggle in, still smiling.

14

"YOU REALLY DON'T expect me to wear that thing, do you?" Jake is staring at his costume as if it might jump up and bite him. "I thought you said *no* dress for me. And seriously, knee socks? And what's with the lame Peter Pan hat and booties?"

"Well, it's clearly not a dress, Jake," Dad tells him. "You'll be wearing hose and knee-breeches on your bottom half. And on your top half, you'll be wearing this tunic, called a doublet, with a jerkin over top. This was usually worn by the working class, but it will work perfectly well for your costume. Now if we wanted to be authentic …"

"Okay, Dad, enough with the fashion history lesson. He'll totally rock this outfit." Jake gives me a scathing eye roll. I smile back at him and say, "Check out my costume."

I hold up a flowing green dress with a tapered waist and billowing sleeves. There's a sweet little cap for my head, like something straight out of *Romeo and Juliet*. I can hardly wait to get ready for the dance tonight.

"Ellie's already got her costume, and she's meeting us at the dance," I explain to Jake. "She came over to the high school with us this morning to pick it out, then we dropped her off at home." I can't help grinning at the thought of how gobsmacked Ellie was when she saw the creepy Banquo costume hanging on the rack. "She figures it might be a good idea to spend some time with her mom today after being allowed to sleep over last night. I hope those two can work on fixing things. Their relationship is so messed up, and they hardly even talk to each other anymore."

"Let's hope she's finally done with that dude," Jake says.

Mom is sitting in an armchair nearby. She's sipping tea and studying Jake with something that might be major approval. I know she's okay with this, whatever it is. When he looks the other way, she gives me the A-OK sign with her finger and thumb as she beams behind her mug. She told me last night after he left that the two of us look adorable together — her words — and that he seems like such a cool guy. I told her not to get her hopes up, that we're just good friends who've bonded over the tragedy of Kit.

But I can't stop thinking about that sweet kiss, that snug and solid hug when he buried his face in my neck. Is it just a friendship thing, a sort of we-totally-get-each-other thing? Or is it, possibly, an honest-to-goodness *real* thing?

DARKNESS DROPS LIKE a stage curtain that evening as Jake and I head for the Sadie Hawkins dance. It's the end of October, and fall has already dug in deep. I'm almost sorry I haven't worn a jacket over my costume, but I didn't want to cover it up and ruin the effect — because it looks totally awesome on me! Even Jake said so. He isn't thrilled about wearing his outfit, though, as he keeps reminding me on the way over.

"Okay, so these dorky stockings and breeches are totally making my legs itch," he says, scratching hard. "How do girls even wear this stuff?"

Which makes me laugh out loud. Wow, he must *really* care about me to step so far out of his comfort zone.

"Guess you should've shaved," I tell him, and I'm sure I hear him growl at me.

We meet all sorts of strange and curious creatures along the way. Movie heroes and villains, TV show characters, and a few wizards and hobbits.

There are way too many superhero duos, and we're glad we didn't pick that. There's lots of the undead, as well. And just to make it completely freaky, many of them are zombie-walking their way toward the school in a moaning, stumbling pack of tattered, blood-soaked rags, dripping faces, and severed limbs. It's like the zombie apocalypse has arrived. Even Aubrey shuffles past us in a complete daze, groaning and slobbering. She doesn't even break character for a second to say hi. Jake sticks out his arms and tries to follow them, until I snatch hold of his elbow and spin him around.

"This way, Macbeth," I say as I drag him toward the school. "Keep an eye open for Banquo's ghost. Fingers crossed that she doesn't chicken out."

"Sure wish *I* was a zombie," he says, then leans over and furiously scratches at his leg again.

In my last few texts from Ellie, she was getting dressed and laughing at herself in the mirror. Then she complained that the costume was going to smudge her makeup, so she decided to shove the whole thing in a bag and change when she got to the school.

Finally around 7:30, as Jake and I mill around checking out cool costumes, she texts, On the way.

Perfect timing, I text back.

The doors are opening at 8:00. For the next half hour, we chat in groups and take photos with our phones. We never show up at dances this early, but tonight's an exception with all the crazy costumes everyone's rocking. Jake's still eyeing the zombies longingly, no matter how many times I jab him in the ribs. We head over to stand in line just before the chaperones begin to admit everyone. I keep checking my phone. I message Ellie when my itchy impatience finally wins out.

U almost here? Doors are about to open!

Getting close. Abt 5 min.

When the doors open, she still hasn't turned up. I stand in line, craning my neck in the direction I expect her to be walking from. But the road leading to the school is deserted, and there's no sign of Ellie under the orange glow of streetlamps.

"Geez, where is she? Can't she ever follow through with anything?"

Jake squeezes my hand. "Quit your worrying, *milady*," he says in his best British accent. "She'll turn up soon enough, just like a bad *halfpenny*."

Somehow Jake can always find a way to make me smile.

Finally they let us storm the gym, and as we surge through the doors, everyone lets out a gasp. The kids on the school social committee have done an amazing job of transforming the space into a haunted graveyard, complete with weathered headstones, severed limbs, eerie, twisted trees with dangling spider webs, and twinkle lights draped everywhere. A spooky crypt, glowing green from inside and spilling fog, dares us to enter at our own risk. The undead brigade stumbles straight in that direction, of course. They're having such a blast that I think most of the rest of us wish we could be zombies, too. The opening song is "Thriller," which makes it even cooler when they break into dance.

I can't focus on anything, though, because after the first couple of tunes, Ellie still hasn't shown up. Should I be worried or angry? No text updates, either, which makes it even weirder. And Jake catches me every time I check my phone.

Finally he wraps one arm around me, then cups my chin in his hand and makes me look straight into his eyes. "Stop obsessing over Ellie and try to have some fun. Geez, Clems, why do you let her get to you even when she's nowhere near you?"

I'm wondering the same thing when my phone buzzes and vibrates in my hand.

"Dare you to ignore that," Jake says. I ignore him instead and check the message.

Meet me in the w/room.

"Okay, she's here, finally." I squeeze his hand. "She wants me to meet her in the washroom. Be right back. And I promise you, for the rest of the night I'll only be obsessed with you, *my worthy lord*."

"I look forward to it, *dear wife*," he says with a chivalrous Shakespearean bow. Then he kisses my hand, and I practically melt like a Popsicle in the sunshine.

The halls are empty except for a few costumed stragglers hurrying toward the gym and a chaperone on patrol.

My footsteps echo off the walls, and they seem to follow me as I pick up my pace.

I hope Ellie won't be pulling one of her lame pouting acts, or crouched on the toilet seat crying like yesterday. I've had enough of that garbage. It's time for her to totally take control of her problems instead of just avoiding them.

I step into the washroom and the door creaks shut behind me.

"Ellie?" My voice bounces off the ceramic and metal. "You in here?" No feet showing under the stall doors. "Quit playing games for god's sake. You're missing a great party!"

Nothing. Fury seethes under my skin, and I feel my face burning. This girl is great at making me crazy. Why did I even give her another chance?

"Okay, that's it. I am *so* done with this messed-up game, Ellie Denton," I tell the walls.

Just as I turn to leave, the door opens.

"Finally. Where were y —"

Banquo's gory ghost steps inside.

And this ghost is way too tall to be Ellie.

"Where's the watch?" the ghost says. In Mac's desperate voice. As he pulls off the hood, it's like all the blood suddenly drains from my body.

"Aren't you supposed to be at some university party, Mac?" I try to disguise a ripple of dread with something that sounds like boldness. "And where's Ellie?"

"Don't worry about Ellie. So are you wearing the watch or what? Because I need to have it. Like, right *now*."

He's standing between me and the doorway. There's no way out of this situation. My only option is to stall and hope Jake comes looking for me. Or to yell, but my voice isn't working so well right now.

"Why would I be wearing a *broken* watch? And why do you need it so badly?" I ask, playing dumb.

"Give me the watch, and maybe I'll tell you." His voice is raw and raspy, his face twitching every which way. "Come on. Let's make this easy."

"I don't have it. Why would you even think I'd wear it to this dance?"

He frowns, and seems confused as he stands there gaping at me. I'm pretty sure Mac doesn't think things through very much. He acts mostly on impulse, roaring around like his muscle car, looking tough on the outside. But what's really happening on the inside? There must be some way to get through to this guy.

"Seriously, tell me why you need it, Mac, and maybe I'll go get it for you."

"I *can't* tell you that, yet."

His face hardens again, and he takes another step forward. But now he looks more like a scared little kid than tough guy. Something is eating at him big time.

"I *know* what went down that night, Mac." I half-whisper so he'll have to listen. "Ellie told me all about it. How Kit caught you guys. How he wanted Ellie's watch and grabbed her wrist. How you *made* her give it to him."

Mac's squinting eyes grow wide. Then, I can't believe it. His face sort of crumples.

"He was pissing us off." He looks down at the floor. When he looks up at me again, his eyes are watering. "He was being such a pest, wouldn't go away, so I did something stupid to try and *make* him go away. I didn't realize he had so many problems, that he was *challenged*. I just thought he was some dumbass giving us a hard time."

"That's not the story Ellie told me!" My heart is slamming in my ribcage. "She said he just ran off with the watch. What did you do, Mac?"

He scrubs at his face. "She's been trying to protect me. All this time. And what would happen if the cops didn't believe my story? Or if Ms. Stitski hears, and tries to nail me for it? I'm supposed to start some college courses in January. If my parents find out, they'll freak, maybe even boot me out of the house. So nobody can ever know about this. That watch has to be gone for good."

Mac leans his back against the wall, and starts sliding down till he's sitting on the floor in a tangle of legs and bed sheets. Then he buries his face in his hands and moans as though something is hurting.

"Okay, so what happened to Ellie? Where is she?"

"I'm right here!"

The washroom door opens. Ellie stands there, breathing hard, face red, the complete opposite of happy.

"Mac, I am so totally sick of all this," she says. "I hate *you*. I hate that *watch*. I hate *everything*."

But then she takes two giant steps forward, sinks to the floor, throws her arms around his neck, and starts sobbing. "Oh, god, I'm so sorry for every crappy thing that's been happening."

And I'm so totally confused that I want to scream.

15

THE TWO OF them huddle in a heap on the washroom floor, hanging on to each other like they're the last people on earth. Mac catches my eye over Ellie's shoulder, and just shakes his head.

"Told you she was messed up, Clems. We *both* are." He hugs Ellie harder, which makes her sob even louder.

"You mean you two … you two actually *like* each other? For real?" I'm in shock.

"Yeah," Mac says. "We do, a *lot*. But there's always this *thing* between us. This lousy thing about Kit, and what happened that very first night we hooked up."

Then it dawns on me. "Wait, so that means you guys set this whole thing up tonight."

"It was my dumb plan, Clems." Ellie looks like a sad clown with her smudgy makeup.

The two of them stand up, arms still entangled, as if they need one another for support.

"But it was mostly my fault," Mac says. "I was pissed when Ellie told me you wouldn't give her back the watch yesterday at your place."

"And I was afraid if I asked you for it again, you'd get *more* suspicious, maybe figure out what Mac did. I even tried to find it in your bedroom last night."

"So *that's* what you were doing. Geez, Ellie, I almost

thought I could trust you again. Huh! Stupid me." I'm
not sure if I want to yell at them or burst into tears. "And
how about when you jumped out of Mac's car yesterday,
acting like you were all freaked out. Then told that story
to me and Jake. Was that all a set up, too?"

"No, that was for *real* Clem. He was scaring me, acting all sketchy, and squeezing my wrist like I told you
yesterday. So I jumped out of his car when it stopped."

"And I'm still sorry about that babe," Mac says, kissing her temple.

"I know that now, Mac. And I totally wanted to try
keeping my distance from him, Clem. Honest! But then
after we turned out the lights in your bedroom he started
texting me again. And at first I ignored him, but he seemed
so scared and desperate that I started texting him back …"

"Right. I saw you texting." I squint at her. "And *then*
what, Ellie?"

"He kept begging me to look for the watch after you
fell asleep. He sucked me right back in. He always does. I
… I can't help it, Clem. That's why I was digging around
in your closet. I was looking for the stupid watch. I didn't
really lose my way in the dark." Mac strokes her hair,
almost tenderly.

I groan and bury my face in my hands.

"I *know* how bad it sounds," she says between hiccup-
ping sobs. "But please, just listen to me one more time,
okay. I let Mac use my costume to get into the school
dance tonight so he could ask you for the watch himself,
maybe even scare you into giving it to him. Everything
is always, *always* about that freaking watch."

Behind us the washroom door slams open.

"Jeez, Clem, you didn't come back, then I heard someone say they saw Banquo's ghost walk by, so I started checking all the ..." Jake stares at us. "What just happened? I have a feeling I missed something."

"I have a feeling we *both* missed something," I say, still glaring at them. "Okay, so what did Mac do? What *was* it?" I'm afraid to hear, but I need to know.

Jake comes over to me and wraps me in his arms, pulling me against his chest so we're both facing Mac and Ellie. It's so good, so comforting, to lean into him like that.

"Tell them, Ellie," Mac says in an almost gentle voice. "How it *really* happened that night."

Ellie lets go of Mac, then heads to the sink and starts splashing cold water on her face. Again with the raccoon eyes.

"You know how stubborn Kit can be. So Mac started sort of shoving him, telling him to get lost, but he wouldn't. So Mac told me to just give him my watch. But I didn't want to because my Nana gave it to me, and I was afraid he might lose it."

I close my eyes and wait for the rest.

"And that's when he did it. Mac grabbed my wrist and pulled off the watch. You know how the strap is elastic. And then he just threw it. Kit totally freaked. He started yelling 'Now Ellie's watch is lost,' and saying that he had to go find it."

"He went ballistic," Mac explains in a thick voice. "Actually started trying to punch me. So I shoved him, and he went stomping off into the dark. I tried to find him but I couldn't. And I *swear* I had no clue he went over the edge." One huge tear slides down his cheek.

"I should have just given him my watch. It's totally my fault that he died." Ellie pounds her fist on the wall.

"But Mac's the one who threw the watch. So it's his fault, too," I tell her.

"But it wouldn't be, if I'd given Kit the watch first! Don't you *get* that, Clem? And Mac doesn't want anyone to ever find out about all this. But it's *killing* me. I had to tell somebody!"

Mac's face is ashen. "I've been freaking out for four months, worrying about that stupid watch and about the truth coming out. My mom wants me to see someone about my bad attitude, as she calls it. My dad won't even talk to me anymore."

"Mac's folks have no clue why he's been in such a lousy mood for so long," Ellie says. "And neither does my mom. But I'm too afraid to talk about it, because it's just so awful."

"Same with me," Mac says. "That watch has been haunting us. *Everything* has. We can't get past it. We can't stop thinking about it or talking about it. And we don't know what to do."

"Wow, déjà vu all over again," Jake whispers, then hugs me even closer.

Mac scrubs his head with his fingertips. Ellie watches him with what might almost be regret. And maybe even a touch of warmth. Then she looks at Jake and me as tears well in her eyes again.

"The very worst part of all is that the whole thing was *both* our faults. We're *both* to blame for what happened to Kit. Neither of us actually pushed him over the edge, but I keep telling Mac that in a way, we both did. We're both responsible. We're *both* murderers, Clems!"Then she buries her face in Mac's chest and starts crying hard all over again.

"This is the way it's been," Mac says. "For four months. Crying, not crying. Liking each other, hating each other. But not being able to walk away from each other. It totally sucks."

I watch them clinging to one another, two more kids like us feeling the sideways damage from that terrible night. Ellie's been a mess ever since, lying to everyone, manipulating me, fighting with her mom, skipping school. Then there's her relationship with Mac, needing to be with him all the time, but constantly fighting. They're both walking disasters.

But now I think I understand why.

Jake and I are definitely not the same as them, but we know what it's like to be haunted by guilt, followed by that horrible shadow.

"You know what, guys," I tell them. "There just might be a way to start fixing this. It's not gonna be easy, but it'll be totally worth it. I'll fill you in right after the dance."

Ellie nods, and then Jake and I leave her and Mac to their sniffles and tears.

ELLIE MAY NOT be crying, but she is definitely not happy when she hears my plan. Her hand is right in my face.

"I absolutely cannot face that family, Clems. There is *no way*."

The four of us are sitting around a table eating burgers and fries in McDonalds after the dance. Mac drove us here in the Wildcat. He stuck around for the rest of the Sadie

Hawkins, dressed as Banquo's ghost. And with a bit of help from the lipstick and liner in Ellie's makeup bag, we managed to turn her into a semi-zombie, with mussed-up hair, smudged up eyes, and dripping blood. Which means that, right now, a *lot* of people in McDs are staring at us, grinning.

"So, you might as well just quit talking about it because it *ain't* happening." Ellie looks at Mac. His face is practically as white as Banquo's. "Mac agrees, I think," she adds. Mac just sits there nodding slowly.

"But *we* did it," I tell them. "Trust me, Jake and I were terrified, but we did it. And Kit's mom wasn't so bad. More sad than mad. But real happy to hear stories about Kit."

"She even made us tea," Jake says.

"But *we* killed her son," Ellie half-shrieks, and a couple of heads turn our way.

"No, you didn't," I tell her. "It was an *accident*. Remember?"

"But if we hadn't been there, it wouldn't have happened at all." Mac pokes at the remains of his Big Mac. He pushes it away. "How can we even look her in the eye?"

I take a deep breath. "Look, I can't stop blaming myself, either. He went looking for a place to pee and never came back. And I never went to check on him. How can I ever forgive myself for *that*?"

"And, god, Clems, I let you just keep on believing it was your fault, so I wouldn't have to confess our part in it." Ellie swallows hard as more tears seep out. "How *can't* you hate me?"

"It hasn't been easy," I admit. "In fact a few times …"

"It's *my* fault he was there." Our heads turn when Jake says that. "He followed me to the quarry, and I let him come. And I didn't check up on him after."

"And if a bunch of kids hadn't planned the field party, *none* of us would have been there," I say, trying to convince myself. "Isn't it just a whole lot of bad timing and bad luck?"

Mac hunches over the table and buries his head in his arms. Ellie rubs his back in slow circles. "We are all horrible people," she murmurs.

I can't even find a good reason to disagree with her.

"Look, we all had our stupid, selfish reasons for doing what we did that night," I tell them. "And nothing will ever bring Kit back. So the best thing I think *we* can do is try to help out his family. Any way we can. So Ms. Stitski will stop trying to find someone to blame, and find a way to move on instead."

"Like how?" Jake asks.

"There's plenty of ways. I'm helping Kevin with school. You guys will think of something. What happened that night is done. What happens next is up to us."

Mac blows out a long slow sigh. Ellie chews on her lip.

"So, what about the watch?" she says. "I don't ever want to see it again. And, god, I sure don't want Kit's mom finding out about it. Imagine what would happen if she did." Ellie's eyes get wide at the thought. "What should we do with it, Clems?"

I've been thinking about that for the whole evening. I've finally made up my mind.

"It's your watch, Ellie. So I guess you should be the one to decide."

Ellie's eyebrows fly up. "Okay, so how about we give it back to Kit?" she says. Clearly she's been thinking about this, too. "Leave it in the last place he ever was, where his spirit might even still be. The quarry pond."

Mac nods. "I have a flashlight in my car. Let's get it over with. We *need* to do this."

"But I don't have the watch on me," I tell them as uneasiness creeps in. "We'd have to go to my place and get it. And my curfew's midnight."

"It's only 11:20," Ellie says. "There's lots of time. Five minutes to your place, ten to the quarry if we hurry. Let's do it. *Please*! I need some closure. This will help."

"But only if you're okay with this, Clems." Jake grabs my hand under the table. "We don't have to do it if it won't work for you."

Ellie and Mac are gazing at me with desperation. I shrug. Then I nod.

WE COULDN'T HAVE picked an eerier night to do the deed. Like, the scare factor of the school's graveyard theme multiplied by a hundred. Floating fingers of fog swirl past the car as Mac steers it along the narrow gravel laneway that ends at the quarry. Tonight the stars are buried behind a thick cloud cover, and beyond the car headlights, the scattered trees and bushes gleam like creepy stick people. I half expect *Macbeth*'s three witches to show up any minute.

Squeezed up against Jake in the back seat, I clutch the watch in my hand. My parents, who were already in bed, didn't even notice when I slipped inside the house to grab it. And the only sound from Zach's room was an annoying video game blasting away.

Now that we're here, I wonder if this was such a great plan after all. But I know it's too late for that, too late to turn back. When Mac cuts the car engine and lights, all around us is dead dark.

"Flashlight. Hurry," I say as Jake and I crawl out of the back seat.

As the fog swirls around us in the flashlight beam, it's like we're walking inside a ghost. I slip my arm through Jake's and pull him closer. Two steps ahead, Ellie lights the path, bouncing the beam off all the landmarks that don't seem so familiar anymore. Mac is glued to her like a shadow as we walk in silence toward the spot where Kit vanished that night.

We all stop near the edge. Ellie dances the light across the black surface of the water. The bright-white circle shifts and splinters like broken shards of moon. I bite the inside of my cheek so I won't burst into tears.

"You're the one who should do this, Ellie," I say, and I hand her the watch.

She pinches it between her finger and thumb like it's something vile.

"I hate this thing," she murmurs, and flings out her arm.

We all hear the splash when her watch hits the water. Afterward, we can't get away from that place fast enough. The car doors slam, Mac's tires spin on the gravel, then the Wildcat bumps and lurches along toward the road.

But then he hits the brakes. There's another car coming at us, and seconds later it stops directly in front of us, blocking our way.

I realize it's a police cruiser just as the two officers are climbing out.

16

MAC SWITCHES OFF the car engine. None of us utter a word. The only sound is our breathing. In the dark I grope for Jake's hand. It's as clammy as mine.

Only one of the officers approaches the car. He taps on the window, while the other one takes down the licence plate then goes back to the cruiser. I figure he's checking it.

"Let me do the talking, okay?" Mac says, just before he cranks the window down.

"Nice car," the officer says. "Is it yours?"

"Grad present from my folks, officer," Mac says in a polite voice as he hands the cop his driver's licence.

"Lucky you." The officer looks at the licence for a moment, then leans through the window and shines a flashlight in our faces, one by one.

"And what are you kids doing out here tonight?" he says. He sniffs, probably looking for the wrong kind of smell: booze on our breaths, a whiff of pot. Satisfied, he backs away.

"Just hanging out after the school dance," Mac tells him.

"A *costume* party, I hope." He grins a bit as he looks us over. "But aren't you a little *old* for a school dance, MacKenzie?"

"It's my girlfriend Ellie Denton's high school, sir." Mac's voice is steady. I have a feeling he's used to answering questions like this.

"Is that you?" he aims the light at Ellie and she squints.

"Uh-huh, I mean, *yes,* officer."

"And you two were at the dance as well?" The light is in our eyes now. We nod.

"So why pick this place?"

"Guess it's sort of a town hangout, sir," Mac says. "We went to McDonalds after the dance, then came here. My friends still had some time left before their curfew."

"And what time's the curfew?"

"Pretty soon. Midnight," Mac tells him.

"Uh-huh, okay." Then he walks back to the cruiser and consults with the other officer. I hear Ellie gasping. It sounds like she's hyperventilating.

"Shhh," Mac says, rubbing her back. "It's all good, stay cool."

He comes back, shines the light on Mac's face again, and hands back his licence.

"Okay, the plate checks out. You should pay that parking ticket though."

"I've been meaning to do that. Sorry, officer."

"You kids *do know* what happened here a few months ago?" the cop says. "Don't you?"

It doesn't really seem like a question, though. Jake squeezes my hand so hard it hurts.

"Yes, sir," Mac says, solemnly. "We all do."

"So were any of you here that night? When Kristopher Stitski died?"

Blaring silence. My whole body is quaking. I want to jump from the car and run.

"Look," the officer says. "I know that nobody wants to talk about it. I get that. But this is a lousy spot to hang out. Somebody *died* here. It's dangerous, treacherous. Don't come here anymore. Got that, everybody?"

"Yes, sir," Mac says.

"And the rest of you?"

"Yes, sir," we all say.

"Good. Now take these kids home, MacKenzie," he says, then raps on the side of the Wildcat before walking back to the cruiser.

Mac lays his head on the steering wheel. In the dim glow from a distant streetlight, I can see his shoulders shaking as Ellie leans against him and rubs his back.

When I start crying, Jake pulls me closer and wipes the tears from my cheeks. I can hear him sniffling, too.

DURING THE SILENT ride home, each of us have our own muddled thoughts messing with our heads. An almost greedy guilt gnaws into my brain, like some ravenous gremlin that's been waiting too long to be fed. When will this feeling ever go away? And how different will I feel if it does?

After Mac drops me off, and I hug everyone goodbye, I break house rules and take my phone to my room. I'm still on edge, and I want to stay connected in case Jake needs to talk. I keep it on vibrate, and hold it in my hand for security while I stare at the ceiling, aware that sleep will be playing hide-and-seek.

My eyes are still wide open when Ellie texts after 2 a.m.

U awake?

Haven't slept yet, I say.

Me either. Too freaked.

I feel sick inside out.

So what happens next?

Wish I could tell you, Els.

Yeah, I know, Clems.

Nite. I switch off my phone and wait for sleep to come find me.

SUNDAY AFTERNOON. I sit at a table in the library feeling all muzzy in the head. The rest of my night was haunted by the guilt gremlin, disturbed by twisted dreams. My eyes opened for the day way too early.

I stayed in my room until late morning, then tried to conjure up a smile when Mom was dishing out pancakes and sausage. I told the family that the dance was fun, and Dad said he didn't even hear me come home. I reassured him that I hadn't broken curfew. He said, no worries, he trusts me, then squeezed my hand. A part of me shrivelled up inside.

I went back to my room until it was time to leave for the library with my brother and meet up with Kevin.

Beside me Zach squirms in his chair. He usually spends Sunday afternoons playing video games, *not* studying. I'm still surprised that he agreed to come.

"Why couldn't we do this at home?" he says.

"Relax. It won't kill you to skip screen time for a change. Go find a book to read or something." I sweep out my arm at the rows of shelves and stacks of books everywhere.

"You sound just like Mom. When are they coming, anyway?"

It's already past two. Ms. Stitski and Kevin are late. I wonder if maybe I should have called to remind them.

When Zach gets bored enough to wander into the children's section, I check my phone. Jake texted me first thing this morning to ask if I was okay. I told him yes, even though I wasn't. When I asked him, he lied, too. I haven't heard from anyone since.

How can any of us *possibly* be okay after last night? I'm being eaten alive by the likelihood that we've made a huge mistake by getting rid of the watch and remaining mute in front of the police officer. He knew. How could he *not* know. The silence inside Mac's car was practically shrieking out our failure to do the right thing.

After all these months, the complete story, with all the puzzle pieces filled in, is finally clear to me. To the four of us. We are sitting on the truth. But how can revealing it make any difference to the outcome? Do Ms. Stitski and Kevin deserve to know, or would that knowledge slice even deeper into their wounds?

"*Is this a dagger which I see before me,*" I murmur. No wonder Lady Macbeth went insane from the guilt.

There's a commotion near the entrance, then Kevin Stitski comes bounding across the library, grinning wide. Behind him his mom, wearing pressed jeans and a matching jacket, crosses the floor in her brisk, efficient way, eyes straight ahead, chin jutting, on a mission.

She's wearing dark, square-framed glasses, and a touch of makeup brightens her face. But she also looks scared. I try not to stare.

"Sorry, we're late," Kevin says. "I had to talk my mom into letting me come. She hardly ever lets me go out alone. So we made a deal, and that's why she's here." He plops down on a chair beside me and flings his backpack on the table. Then he starts hauling out books.

A hand touches my shoulder. I look up into Ms. Stitski's gleaming eyes. Tears. She leans in closer.

"Thanks for doing this, Clem." Her voice is soft, and it quavers. "It means a lot, and it's so good for Kevin. He's so resilient. I envy that."

"You need to get out more, Ma. Instead of just working twenty-four-seven," he says, then looks at me. "So where's your brother anyway?"

I point. "Go get him, and we'll get this party started."

As Kevin lopes over to Zach, his mom watches him go. Her face is furrowed in all the worry places, deep grooves between her eyebrows and around her mouth. It reminds me of when I make a crazy face, and my grandma warns me that if the wind blows, it'll stay that way. I have a feeling Ms. Stitski has spent far too much time lately thinking nasty thoughts.

"So, I heard from the police this morning, Clem," she says. "Apparently someone in McDonalds last night overheard a group of kids in costumes talking about Kit. The police picked one of them up. I'm headed over to the station right now to find out more about it."

I'm pretty sure my heart stops dead for a second, before it starts beating double-time. *Who, what, when, where, why?* my mind screams. But I try to act all cool and nonchalant.

"Oh, really?" I say, summoning a smile.

"I haven't said anything in front of Kevin yet, though," she adds almost like a warning. "I don't want him finding out about this latest turn of events until I know what's going on."

My smile is wrestling to stay in place. "Well, maybe this could be a good thing. Maybe they've turned up new evidence that will help you and Kevin find some closure. Don't worry, I'll make sure he gets home safely when we're done here."

Ms. Stitski squints her eyes. "Don't worry about it. His aunt will pick him up outside the library at around four, Clem. I'll see you later."

My mouth goes totally dry as I watch her walk out the library door. I dig a water bottle out of my backpack and take a huge swig. My mind goes into rewind, trying to recall who was sitting nearby in McDs last night, who could have overheard us talking. It could have been anybody.

How the heck can I possibly focus on anything else until I find out?

Kevin follows Zach back to the table like a puppy dog. Then he looks around.

"Where's my mom? Hiding behind some shelves watching me? She always needs to know exactly where I am. It's making me crazy."

"She left," I tell him. "Your aunt is picking you up around four."

"Seriously? Wow, that's progress, I guess." He plops down in a chair. "This is so cool. I get to study with Zach Sanford. I can't wait to tell all my friends."

"Seriously?" I ask. "You actually think my little brother is *cool*?"

"Everybody does," Kevin says, grinning.

"Wow. He sure hides it well."

Zach shoots me a sneer then he sits down, too. Kevin scoots his chair closer to him. Zach rolls his eyes, but I can tell he enjoys having a fan.

"Okay, so clearly you're at different levels," I say. "How*ever*, since Zach is three years ahead of you, Kevin, he'll be able to help you out with your work after I help him out with his. It'll be a good refresher course for him."

"What?" Zach says. "I didn't sign up for *this*, Clem." Kevin's face sags. Zach notices. "But, whatever. Maybe it'll even do me good." Kevin grins again.

"Trust me, it definitely will," I tell him.

My phone vibrates in my backpack. I've secretly vowed not to look at that screen while I'm working with the guys. I try to ignore it, but it buzzes again. Zach smirks, daring me.

"I can do this, you know," I tell him.

"Yeah, right," he says. "Anyway, I don't care if you check your phone, Clems. The library doesn't fall under house rules, right?"

"Exactly," I say, then whip out my phone.

I read Ellie's text message three times.

Mac got picked up by the cops. His dad called me.

What is HAPPENING, I text back.

Don't know. I'm scared. ttyl

I go into a daze and stare off across the room. My imagination spins in every direction as I try to decide how any revelations by Mac could change things. There's a strange humming in my head, like white noise switching on in my brain. The buzz of a dozen possibilities, a dozen scenarios, a dozen awful endings to this story.

Is Mac at the police station right now, waiting to tell the officers, and Ms. Stitski, everything he knows? And what will that mean for us?

Finally, somebody else will know. Finally, the police can decide what to do next. Maybe it will help kill some of my guilt and I won't have to be fixated on that "horrible shadow" anymore.

But then again, will I be implicated in some way, along with Jake and Ellie? Will we all be held to blame for Kit's death? Will we all be charged as accessories?

It could turn out to be a good thing, like I said to Ms. Stitski. It could be closure for the police, and maybe even for some of the other kids who were at the quarry. There have to be more out there, blaming themselves like we are. Surely others connected with Kit that night, found their own opportunities to look out for him. And didn't, for one reason or another, just like the four of us. But when I think of Ms. Stitski, about to hear what really happened, I think of something else, too. It could also be a very bad thing. For the two people closest to Kit. And it could go either way for them and for us. And if it turns out that nobody's charged, will Ms. Stitski just keep on blaming herself forever?

"Hey, Clems. You lost in space again?" Zach nudges my shin under the table. "Let's get started already, before me and Kevin ditch you to go home and play video games."

Kevin beams. Zach grins. I force myself to focus on the moment.

17

IT TAKES AN enormous effort to sit still through two hours of tutoring while trying to ignore my latest dilemma. Turning off my phone helps me stay in the moment. I don't *want* any updates. I'm afraid to find out what might happen next.

So I block out everything awful and focus on the guys to make sure they actually learn something, and that it actually sinks in. Then I even wander around the library for a bit, browsing the shelves, to let my brother do it on his own. In the end the afternoon is totally worth it because of how well Kevin and Zach hit it off.

When we finish up around four o'clock, Kevin actually hugs me after he slings his backpack over his shoulder.

"Thanks. You guys really helped me out today. Hope we can do it again some time." Then he looks at me sideways with a half-smile. "My mom's glad you and Jake dropped by that day, you know. I think it made her feel better about a bunch of stuff. She thought nobody cared about Kit, but I keep trying to tell her that everybody did. I wish she'd quit asking questions and looking for answers, though. There's no point anymore." He shrugs. Then he looks at Zach with hopeful eyes. "See ya around school, I guess, huh?"

My brother gives Kevin a high-five, and grins. "Yep, later, dude."

"See," I say to Zach as we watch Kevin push through the library exit. "That wasn't so bad after all, was it?"

"Nope. I can think of way worse stuff. Anyway, Kevin's kind of a cool little guy. Maybe I'll take him to a movie some time, or something."

"You're kind of a cool guy yourself, bro," I say. "I'm totally proud of you for helping me out and chilling with Kevin today." When I try to squeeze his shoulder he shoves my hand away and gives me an eye roll.

"Geez, don't push it, Clems," he says, but from the sloppy grin on his face, I know he feels pretty good on the inside.

As I ride my bike home from the library, trailing far behind my brother, a sense of doom begins to crowd out the warm glow from helping Kevin. By the time I walk inside with a fake smile plastered across my face, alarm bells are ringing in my head. I can already hear Zach's video game blasting away in the family room.

"Zach said it went great." Mom beams at me as she chops a carrot.

Dad is scrubbing potatoes at the sink. "You two did a good thing today," he says.

"Yeah, guess so. Got some school stuff of my own to get done before dinner." And I rush past them before they can start asking any more questions.

I need to make some notes for my revue theme presentation in theatre arts tomorrow. But I barely have enough energy to flop down on my bed and stare at the ceiling. It's nearly impossible to concentrate on anything else but Ellie's last text. *Mac got picked up by the cops.*

I've felt haunted for months, but now I'm being stalked by a different sort of dread. A swarm of what-ifs followed me home from the library, and they continue to hover in the air like a cloud of mosquitoes. Biting at me, making me itch with a restless anxiety.

What if the police want to talk to the rest of us? And we all tell different stories.

What if they go diving for that watch at the bottom of the pond? And find it.

What if we're accused of tampering with evidence? And charged.

The more I dwell on it, the worse I feel. I don't even have the courage to turn my phone on in case there's another message waiting to scare the heck out of me. But I need to talk to someone, and I decide to phone Jake. He answers on the first ring.

"God, what took you so long, Clem?"

"Yeah, my phone's been off. Ellie let me know about Mac while I was at the library with Kevin and Zach. I couldn't even think straight after she texted. I still can't. What's going to happen to us Jake?" I feel like I'm about to run out of air.

"Calm down," he says. "Hopefully nothing. How did the library go, anyway?"

I figure it's a distraction tactic. But as I start to tell him how well it turned out, my heart slows down, and I feel a bit of a glow again.

"Awesome," Jake says. "I'm kind of working on an idea myself. I know how much Kevin is into skateboarding.

Maybe he'd like some free private lessons or something. I'd have to okay it with his mom first, though."

Just hearing the resolve in Jake's voice finally helps me summon up a smile. He seems to have reached the same place as me in all this awfulness. "I'm sure he'd *love* that Jake," I say. "And so would his mom."

"Hope you're right." Then a long, scary pause. "Okay, so listen. I already know a bit about what happened with Mac and the cops. Ellie texted me. I didn't want to call and bug you about it while you were tutoring. And I've been trying to reach you since just after four but …"

"*What* happened?" My heart is instantly back in overdrive and my smile shrivels up. "What *aren't* you telling me, Jake?"

"I still don't know that much. Only that someone recognized Mac in McDs. And told the cops what they heard us talking about, and about the weird costumes we were wearing. And I guess that officer who talked to us at the quarry after we …"

My insides crumple up like tinfoil. "… after we got rid of the watch. *He's* the one who put it all together, right? How could he possibly forget us? He would have known right away who we were when someone showed up with information. Why haven't the cops picked you and me up yet? Or are they about to? God, what's happening, Jake?"

Jake's momentary silence makes me feel even sicker inside. I almost want to scream.

"Look, I don't even know myself yet. Hopefully nothing is happening. Ellie wants us to meet up with her and Mac tonight around 7:30 at Tim Hortons. You okay with that?"

"This isn't going away any time soon, is it?"

"Maybe it never will, Clems," Jake tells me.

That is the absolute last thing I want to hear him say.

"HELLO IN THERE. Anybody home, Clementine?"

Dad is knocking on the kitchen table as I stare into my plate of pot roast and veggies floating in gravy. It's totally turning my stomach. When I glance up, all three of them are watching me with strange looks. Zach raises one eyebrow like a question mark.

"*Huh*? Did I miss something? What's going on?" I say. I take a tiny bite of meat and chew it slowly.

"We thought maybe you could tell us that," Mom says with narrowed eyes. "You seem so distracted right now, honey. You haven't heard a word we've said all through dinner."

"I just don't feel like talking, I guess. Lots on my mind." My throat is so tight I can hardly swallow.

"Then maybe it would help if you talked about it," Dad says, patting my hand, looking way too concerned about me.

"Probably *not*." I yank my hand away and eat one pea. I can sense them all exchanging glances, even though my head is down.

"Well, why not give it a try anyway?" Mom says in a gentle voice.

I jump to my feet and my chair hits the floor. "Can't you *please* just leave me *alone*?" I snap. "God, I totally miss having our phones on at the table. At least then I didn't have to answer your stupid questions all the time."

As I stomp out of the kitchen I hear Zach telling our parents to just let me go.

In my room, I flop on my bed and bury my head under a pillow.

Without a doubt, everything will come out now. All the nasty lies, the scary truths, and everything else that's been festering away inside the four of us.

Everyone will know we're to blame for Kit's death, and even if nothing happens to us, we'll be shunned by everyone who knows us. Everyone who knew Kit.

How will I even be able to face anyone now? What will my family think? Hot tears ooze out onto my pillow. In the distance I can hear someone's ring tone playing a familiar movie tune. Zach's. A few seconds later there's a knock on my door.

"*What?*" I yell into my pillow. "Go *away!*"

"Ms. Stitski called my phone, Clem," Zach says.

Oh no. "But why does she even have your number?"

"Because I gave it to Kevin at the library today. In case he needs more help."

I sit bolt upright, throw my pillow at the wall. "Tell her I'm busy," I say, scrubbing at my wet cheeks.

"Probably not a good plan," Zach says beyond my door. "She sounds really stuck on talking to you, like right now. Says it's urgent."

My whole body feels extra heavy as I cross my bedroom. Like walking through waist-deep water. I open my door and Zach hands me his phone. Behind him I can see my parents craning their necks in the kitchen.

"Thanks," I say and slam my door in his face.

"Hello?" My voice is barely a whisper.

"Clementine. It's Joan Stitski." Her words are sharp and curt.

"I know."

"Your friend Mac talked to the police."

My friend? "I know."

"I found some things out. Things I never knew before today."

"I figured that might happen," I say.

"I think we should get together and talk," Ms. Stitski says. "About a *lot* of things." It almost sounds as though her voice is trembling with anger. It's a terrifying sound.

I swallow hard. "Okay. How about tonight? Seven forty-five at Tim Hortons?"

"That's fine. I'll see you then," she says, and the line goes dead.

Perfect. If I have to face the wrath of Ms. Stitski again, there's no way I'm doing it without my *friends* beside me.

18

"OKAY, SO TELL us exactly what you told the police today," I say to Mac, keeping my voice low. "Just cut to the chase."

He stares at me across the table. Maybe I jumped the gun by starting my interrogation without any small talk. But I'm in a hurry for him to begin. She'll be walking in on us any time now. Nobody else knows she's coming. Not even Jake. There's a perfectly logical reason for that. I don't want to scare them all off.

"No 'hello' or anything, Clems? I can't believe you guys even beat us here," Mac says.

"Me, neither, since you guys came in a car," I tell him. "So what's the story?"

"Why do you sound so mad?" Ellie asks. "Mac did a good thing today, didn't he?"

"We're not sure about that yet," Jake says.

"Trust me. It's only good news." Mac sips his coffee and grins in a smug way. Ellie snuggles up to him and squeezes his arm, then kisses his cheek. "The cops have *no* plans for opening up the inquiry again. Because there's …" he makes air quotes, "'insufficient information to justify reopening the case.' I memorized that." Another grin.

Ellie giggles like a crazy person, grabs his neck and hugs him harder.

"But what did you *tell* them?" I drum my fingertips on the tabletop and tap my foot. Under the table, Jake puts his hand on my leg to calm me down.

"Well, I told them I was there that night. And that Ellie and I saw Kit just before he disappeared. That we were probably the last ones to see him. That after he ran into us, he just ran away into the dark because he had to take a pee."

My story. "You borrowed *my* story for the police?" I say. "You *lied* to them?"

"It's not exactly a lie, Clem. It's the truth." Mac lowers his eyes and fiddles with his stir stick. "Kit actually did run off because he had to pee."

"But you must have told them more. That can't be the end of it. Didn't they ask you any questions? Any at all?"

Mac snaps the stir stick. "Yeah, well they asked me if I know Spencer. And I said, yeah, I do know him."

"And?" Jake says, leaning forward. "What *else*?"

Mac's dark, narrow eyes stare into Jake's wide blue ones. "Don't worry, dude. I didn't throw him under the bus. They asked me if he was nearby when I watched Kit walk away, and I told them no, the last I saw of Spencer, he was partying by the fire."

Jake's face seems to soften a bit then. One less person who has to worry about being a suspect. One more person who can start to breathe easier now. I'm sure Jake can hardly wait to tell his skateboarding buddy; he's probably itching to text him right away.

"Okay, well, that's cool, I guess," Jake says.

"Yeah, I guess it is," I tell him. "Anything else, Mac?"

"Nope. That's it, man. That's all I told them." Mac just shrugs.

"You mean you left the watch part out completely?" Ellie is staring at him and her wide eyes are brimming with tears. "I thought you *told* the cops about the watch. So we could *all* get past it and move on."

Mac's slow smile reminds me of the Grinch. "What *about* the watch? *What* watch?"

Awkward silence at our table. Like we're all afraid to speak. So he left out the part about the watch. But the watch is at the bottom of the lake now, so what does it even matter anymore? Suddenly it feels as if a huge rock has been lifted off my chest.

Ellie jumps to her feet. Her cup tips over, sending milky coffee pooling on the table, dripping onto the floor. Clearly she's not as over it as I am. Her watch must still symbolize something, at least to her. Jake and I throw our serviettes over the spreading puddle as Ellie stares at Mac.

"Why did you have to leave that part out? I thought you said you told them *everything*. I thought that meant that we were okay now. That the cops understood about the watch."

"We *are* okay," Mac says. "I thought about it a lot. What good will it do if they know about the watch? It won't change anything, will it? It'll only make Kit's mom even crazier, the way I see it. If she ever finds out about that watch, she'll *never* let it go."

Ellie's mouth is half open as she stares at him. "I swear, sometimes I don't even know who you are anymore, Mac." Then the drama queen whirls around and walks straight out the door without even giving him a second look.

"Why's she so pissed?" Mac looks at us, totally perplexed. "I seriously thought this would change everything. For all of us. I thought I did the right thing."

Did he? I know I feel a ton lighter now, and I figure Jake probably does too. But I don't have a chance to ask him. Ms. Stitski is here and she's scanning the room. Mac and Jake spot her at the same instant she finds me.

"What the...?" Jake says, and I grab his hand under the table.

Mac is on his feet, looking like a cornered rabbit searching for an escape route.

"Sit down," I tell him. "I asked her to meet us here. So just shut up, and let me do the talking for a change."

The two guys stare at me, stunned. Ms. Stitski approaches the table and looks at all of us, one by one. She starts nodding as she sits down in Ellie's vacant chair.

"So, this is what it's come to," she says, gazing straight into my eyes. "You set this up, didn't you, Clementine?"

"These guys had no idea you were coming tonight," I tell her.

Ms. Stitski looks at Mac. Her face is dispassionate, completely unreadable. The perfect lawyer.

Mac sips from his cup, trying to look cool, trying to meet her stare with the same sort of blank expression. His fingers twitching on the table give him away.

"I was behind the two-way mirror today," she tells him.

Mac chokes on a mouthful of coffee.

"I heard everything you told the police. I watched your expression the entire time. I wondered what you might be hiding from them."

Mac gulps and his nostrils flare slightly.

"I'm still wondering if you're trying to protect that Spencer character." She practically spits out his name. "I heard he was giving Kit a hard time that night, but there was never enough proof to take it any further, to press charges." Suddenly, she looks as if she's having trouble holding on to her confidence. Her chin is visibly trembling. "And it makes me so sad …" she gulps hard. "*So sad* to think that he might have been treated in such a cruel way, with other kids laughing at him, just before he …"

"No! It didn't happen that way." Jake's deep and solid voice seems to bring her back to the present. "There was never any fight. After Spencer tripped him, Kit just sat there on the grass. And he *laughed*. Really loud and hard. And then everyone else did, too, and some kids helped him back to his feet. And then someone called Spencer an a-hole. They all stuck up for Kit. Honestly. I was there. I saw it happen."

Two tears seep out and trickle down Ms. Stitski's cheeks. "Please, tell me you're not just saying that to make me feel better?" she says.

"I swear, that's exactly how it happened," Jake tells her. "Clem was there, too. You saw it, didn't you Clem?"

I nod out a lie. I was watching Jake, not Spencer and Kit.

She turns to Mac. "Did you see it happen, too?"

Mac looks down at his coffee cup. "Uh, no, I guess I missed it."

Her eyes narrow again. "Why did you miss it? Where were *you*?"

He doesn't answer, so I do. "Mac's embarrassed to tell you, Ms. Stitski," I say. "He was making out with someone. Where nobody could see them."

"Right, you told the police you were with a girl named Ellie. And that Kit went running past you looking for somewhere to go to the bathroom." Then she turns to me.

"But where did he go from there? That's what nobody seems to know." She places her long, pale hands very flat on the table and stares at them. Now it's time for her to hear the rest of the story. I'm sick of keeping this secret any longer.

I focus on my Iced Cap. "The truth is, Ms. Stitski, I think that I might have been one of the last ones to see him, too. He told me he had to … to go to the bathroom. I told him he'd have to do in the bushes, so he walked off into the bushes. And I guess that's when he met up with Ellie and Mac and … and asked them the same question. I think he was embarrassed, afraid that someone might see him peeing. When he didn't come back, I thought he just went home." Another tear gets away on me.

"And you didn't even think to *check*?" Almost a growl. She lowers her head on the table and buries her face in her elbow, as if she's terribly tired all of a sudden. "At least I know that much now," says her muffled voice. Then she looks at us again over her arm. "Anyone else have anything they'd like to share?"

Jake coughs softly. "Okay, Ms. Stitski, there's something else I think you deserve to know. When Kit left home that night, the first person he met was me. The quarry isn't that far from your house. I was on my skateboard, and I just randomly met him walking along the road." Jake's breathing as if he's been running.

Kit's mother stares hard at Jake, blinking fast. "And you just let him *follow* you? You didn't even think that maybe something could go terribly wrong, just knowing that he was …" She slaps the table and Jake's face falls.

"I can't even tell you how sorry I am …" Jake's voice fades away. His chin trembles.

Ms. Stitski inhales deeply. "That part doesn't even matter now, does it? Who am I kidding? He heard about it, he wanted to go, and he went. Straight out the back door after I was in bed, working on my laptop. I didn't even realize he was gone until the morning." She swallows hard. "The fact is, it's mostly my fault. I've just been in complete denial."

"No, Ms. Stitski. It's not your fault," I whisper. "It's nobody's fault. It's just something that happened."

When her eyes meet mine she forces a smile and pats my hand. I can almost hear the watch ticking. It reminds me of that Edgar Allan Poe short story we studied at school, *The Tell-Tale Heart*. It was about a heart that went on beating, even after its owner had been killed. It drove the murderer crazy. But we aren't murderers. None of us. Just a bunch of kids who were in the wrong place at the wrong time, much like Kit himself. And as I sit there watching Ms. Stitski process everything we've just told her, I decide that Mac is right after all. That's it's okay for me to be relieved. I'm sure Jake is too. And that deep down Ellie probably is and she just can't admit it yet. The watch belongs at the bottom of the pond forever. With Kit's spirit.

This part of the story is over. Ms. Stitski, Kevin, all four of us, we need to find a way to move on.

Ms. Stitski slowly rises to her feet. She looks tired and defeated.

"Kevin's waiting in the car," she says. "He has no idea what I'm doing in here. I'd better grab him a box of Timbits and a chocolate milk, don't you think?"

We all nod.

"And thanks for helping him out at the library today, Clem. He's over the moon, you know. And he really likes your brother."

"That's cool," I say. "Zach really likes him. He'd like to take him to the show some time. And keep helping him with schoolwork, too, if that's okay with you?"

Her weary face seems softer now, and her grateful smile reaches her eyes as she nods.

"Do you think Kevin might like skateboarding lessons some time?" Jake throws it out there, just takes a chance and does it. I want to hug him.

"Hmm, let me think about that one," she says. "I guess it would be good for him. Maybe for me, too. I need to give him some space. Give me a call next week." She digs into her purse and hands Jake a business card. Then she heads over to the counter to place her order.

Someone pushes through the entrance just then. Ellie. She looks as if she's seen a ghost as she shuffles to our table, keeping one eye on Kit's mother the entire time.

"I was waiting outside," she says. "I saw her go in when I was leaving. What happened?"

Mac reaches out and catches her hand, pulls her closer to him, hugs her hard.

"Sit down, babe," he whispers. "And I'll tell you everything."

Jake and I look at each other. Then we pick up our takeout cups and walk through the door without even looking back.

19

WE STROLL SLOWLY home, holding hands, a half-moon peering over our shoulders. We talk about what just happened, and what should happen next.

We agree that Mac made the right choice after all. It makes sense that dredging up the watch at this point would only open deeper wounds for Ms. Stitski and confuse Kevin even more. After everything she learned today, she will have to realize that blaming herself or anyone else is pointless. Kit is gone. All the probing and questioning and investigating in the world will never change that sad truth. It's time for her to put away the backpack in the corner, once and for all. We hope she'll be able to do it.

We also realize that even though the watch is gone, we'll always have to live with the memory of Kit and what happened that night. Kind of like a permanent scar on the inside. We'll just have to do our best to dull the pain of our mistakes by remembering our lost friend, and by trying to make things better. For ourselves and for the Stitskis.

When we get home, Jake kisses me for a long time in the dark beside the garage, where nobody will spot us. I kiss him back, and I don't want him to leave. Eventually he hugs me hard, then lopes off.

I float in a daze through the front door, but then my spirits come crashing down hard. All three of them are sitting there, waiting for me in the family room. When I step in, Dad shuts off the TV and crosses his arms.

"I think we all deserve some sort of an explanation for your behaviour tonight, Clem," he says, then points to the empty spot beside him on the sofa. I walk over and sit down slowly.

My mom seems to be on the verge of crying. And even Zach, who usually loves nothing more than to give me a hard time, has a sombre expression.

"Honey, we don't understand," Mom begins. "You're acting so strange lately. Not paying attention to anything we say, always distracted, angry a lot of the time. You're like a yo-yo. Up one minute and down the next." Her hand strays to her neck. "We're very worried, you know."

I give them a wavering smile.

"It's a long story. I only hope you'll listen, right up to the end, and that you'll try hard to understand how and why it all happened."

Then I start deconstructing all the lies, starting right from the very first one, when I went to the quarry that night without ever telling them. I hadn't realized how many had piled up like a giant Jenga tower, until I started pulling them all apart. It was a bit intimidating to catch the looks on my parents' faces: complete disbelief, some disappointment, even a bit of horror. Zach was different, though. It was all news to him, the kid who thinks he knows so much about me. He didn't tear his eyes away for one second. At times he looked as if he wondered if I really *was* his sister.

I stop at tonight, at the Tim Hortons part and our meeting with Ms. Stitski. And even though I've managed to come clean about all the falsehoods I've been feeding them since June, and all the guilt I've been carrying around with me, I leave one part out. The part about the watch. Because it's not really my story to tell.

"I don't even know what to say," Dad says, shaking his head when I'm done. "You should have been willing to talk things over, Clem. To be honest about your guilty feelings, if you thought it was all your fault. It must have been haunting you all these months."

You can't even imagine. But no way I'm going there. I give him a slight nod, instead. "It was haunting all of us, Dad. But we finally all got together and found a way to resolve it. It's really about helping Ms. Stitski and Kevin, isn't it? Helping them move forward."

Mom is still staring, hand still clutching her neck. "I thought I knew you, Clem. I really did. Yet all this … this awfulness was going on, and you kept it hidden from us."

"But you *do* know me, Mom," I say. "Just not *every little thing* about me."

Mom almost looks hurt. "Well, I'd like to think I do," she says. "I'd also like to think you'd share everything with us, all your triumphs, as well as your concerns. And your troubles, too."

"Come *on*. I'm sure you kept some secrets from your parents when you were my age. I bet you didn't tell your mom every single time you kissed a guy, or what you were really doing when you missed a curfew."

Dad has a crooked grin. He nods a bit, and when Mom frowns at him, he shrugs.

"She makes a good point, Laura," he tells her.

"Hmmm," Mom says. "I think I'll need to think that one over a bit before I can offer you a response, John." She waggles a finger at him and they smile at each other in a mysterious way.

Zach looks at me and smirks. "You totally made out with Jake tonight," he says. "Didn't you. I can tell by your face."

And even though my face starts sizzling right up to my ears, I feel like hugging my brother. Because finally, *finally* everyone starts to laugh.

After that I make my exit and head straight for my room. And with so much on my mind, I fear I might lie awake for hours, but somehow sleep finds me quickly. That night I have one of the best nights in ages. No thrashing under the covers, no wrestling gremlins, no drowning nightmares. Just good, old-fashioned, deep-and-delicious zzzzzs.

FIRST THING MONDAY morning, Ellie is on my mind. I haven't heard from her since we walked out of Tim Hortons last night and left her behind with Mac. My fingers are crossed that she'll be smart enough to show up at school this morning. That she might finally have come to her senses after all the craziness of the past few months. She needs to get herself back on track, with school, with her mom, and with her life. And if Mac is still going to be a part of that, I hope that maybe he won't have such a powerful and mesmerizing grip on her any more.

She's already waiting at my locker. Leaning against it, hunched into herself. She doesn't see me coming until I'm standing right in front of her waiting for her to move. She offers me a weary sort of smile and shifts to the right.

"You made it on time today," I say as I spin in my combination. "Yay for you."

"Yeah," she says. No makeup this morning, and a bleary-eyed dullness, probably from lack of sleep. "I made sure. So, Clems?"

"What's up?" I dig through my locker, not willing to look at her in case she's about to throw a brand-new surprise at me.

"I'm so sorry I dragged you into all this." When she touches my arm, I look her straight in the eye.

"Are you *really*? You've said a lot of stuff lately, Ellie."

"I honestly am. I swear, I had no clue that Mac was going to swipe your story. I was as shocked as you were. Then he told me everything that happened with Ms. Stitski. I don't even know what to think about that. And I guess it's okay, after all, that he left out the watch part."

"Jake and I talked about it. And we think we're all right with it too. Maybe Mac wasn't so off base, after all, for what he did. And he helped save Spencer, too."

Ellie looks half-uncertain, half-hopeful. "Really? You know, he's been calling and texting me ever since he dropped me off at home last night. But I decided to ignore him, and to copy your family and switch my phone off. I think I might be done with him this time. I mean, he actually *believes* he solved the problem for all of us."

"He's the one who has to live with himself," I tell her. "Because he really *was* the last one to ever lay eyes on Kit. And I *know* you're not done with him yet, either. You like him way too much to just ditch him. It's so obvious."

"Oh, god, I know. You're totally right, Clems. Seriously, I miss him tons already. I'm texting him right after next period. I'm going to change, for the better though, I promise you. Fix things with my mom, too. But I still don't know how I'll be able to live with *myself*. How I can ever get past what I did that night?" Her eyes are begging for an answer.

"I already told you how. You have to go over there. You have to face them, share your best memories of Kit. Tell them how much you liked him."

"I really *did* like him, so much." Ellie's face is soft and crumpled. "I loved it when we did that Circle of Friends thing with him, you know? It's just that when we got to high school, Kit became more distant. Or maybe it was the rest of us who did. He sort of got lost in the crowd. He was only in one of my classes, instead of all of them, like in middle school. By the end of ninth grade I hardly ever saw him or talked to him."

"You're telling all this to the wrong person," I remind her.

"Okay, Clems. I promise, I'll consider visiting the Stitskis," she offers me a shaky smile. "Even though the thought of it scares the crap out of me."

"I know how you feel," I say, reaching for my books.

"So, did you come up with any half-decent ideas for the revue?" Ellie asks, changing the subject.

"Yup. And, actually, I think we should do one about Kit."

"Really? Hmmm." Ellie frowns. Then her glum face morphs into a smiling one. She follows me toward the auditorium just as the bell rings over our heads.

We all gather on the stage as usual. I have no real game plan. I'm going to wing it. When it's my turn to present, I'll just make it up on the spot, tell Ms. Raven and the rest of the class my idea for the revue theme. I haven't had a lot of time lately to make notes, and I didn't even bring them along today. But they're still scribbled in my head, and I can only hope that they'll come out sounding cool instead of lame.

I let everyone else go ahead of me. The other four ideas are quirky, creative, and fun, which makes mine feel like a huge downer.

When Ms. Raven says, "Anyone else?" I don't even move.

Until I hear Ellie's voice. "I think Clem has a cool idea, Ms. Raven."

When the drama teacher nods at me, I stand up. I look around at everyone, sprawled there on the stage, waiting for me to share my idea.

I take a deep breath, fill up my lungs …

"Okay, so everyone remembers Kit Stitski, right?" Everyone nods enthusiastically. "Well I think this could be a cool way of honouring him. In sketches and song and dance. Call it *The Kit Stitski Revue*. Cause he loved all that stuff, and being on stage, too. And we could invite Ms. Stitski and Kit's brother Kevin as special guests. We could use a sort of 'time' theme. There's tons of material out there related to time. Because Kit was obsessed with it. And as it turned out, we never did get to spend enough time with him. Did we?"

I take another deep breath then sit down. The ghost of an idea. That's all I've got.

One person starts clapping. When I look over, Ellie is sitting there nodding her approval. When I glance at Ms. Raven, she's beaming. Then she starts to clap.

And then, everyone else on the stage does, too.

I CANNOT WAIT to be alone with Jake. Sunday night behind the garage is stuck in my mind like gum on my shoe. I swear the time is ticking backwards all day long. I don't even get to see him during lunch because he has to work on a group science project in the library. I even walk past the library door a few times, just to try to peek inside and catch a glimpse of him. Pathetic.

He's waiting at my locker when I get there after school, though. Leaning against it, with a wide and lazy smile. Jake is waiting for *me*. I still want to pinch myself. Even more when he pulls me up close and kisses my forehead. I snuggle right into his arms like I belong there.

"I missed you," he says close to my ear, and every goose bump on my body prickles.

"Me, too. *So* much." I'm still not sure about all this. About where Jake and I are going, or about what we're leaving behind.

And who knows? Maybe throughout our lives we'll all have some secrets that we need to keep close. Not just to protect ourselves, but to protect the other people in our circle of family and friends who could be even more damaged by them than we are.

Jake told me a secret out by the garage last night, very close to my ear, something that nearly made my heart stop. And I'm never, ever telling. Because it was just for me.